CHALK'S AWAY!

(Even More) School Diaries of Morris Simpson, M.A.

'We trained hard but it seemed that every time we were beginning to form up into teams, we would be reorganised. I was to learn later in life that we tend to meet any new situation by reorganising, and a wonderful method it can be for creating the illusion of progress, while producing confusion, inefficiency and demoralisation.'

Caius Petronius, AD 66 (attrib.)

Morris Simpson's earlier school diaries are also available in the following chronological order:

Class Struggle: The Probationary School Diaries of Morris Simpson, MA 0 340 58420 3

Chalked Off! The School Diaries of Morris Simpson MA 0 340 54363 9

Absolutely Chalked Off! The Further School Diaries of Morris Simpson MA 0 340 56188 2

John Mitchell taught English in Paisley for five years and is now field sales manager for the educational publishing division of Hodder & Stoughton. He also contributes regular articles to the *Times Educational Supplement Scotland*, most particularly Morris Simpson's School Diary, upon which this book is based.

CHALK'S AWAY!

(Even More) School Diaries of Morris Simpson, M.A.

JOHN MITCHELL

Foreword by Jack McLean

Drawings by Weef

Hodder & Stoughton

Published in association with

TIMES EDUCATIONAL SUPPLEMENT SCOTLAND

Acknowledgements

I'd like to thank everyone who's already been thanked in the three previous books. If you want to know who they are, buy them! Plus Harry Brash for the title of this one. Thanks, Harry!

John Mitchell, July 1993

British Library Cataloguing in Publication Data
Mitchell, John
Chalk's Away!: (Even More) School Diaries
of Morris Simpson, M.A.
I. Title
823.914 [F]

ISBN 0 340 60107 8

First published 1993
Impression number 10 9 8 7 6 5 4 3 2 1
Year 1998 1997 1996 1995 1994 1993

Filmset by Wearset, Boldon, Tyne and Wear
Printed in Great Britain for the educational publishing division of Hodder and Stoughton Ltd, Mill Road, Dunton Green, Sevenoaks, Kent TN13 2YA by Cox & Wyman Ltd, Reading

Foreword

From the very first I liked Morris Simpson. I mean, I knew he was an absolute wanker, but I still liked him. Now I have come to admire him. How Morris can maintain his idiocy is beyond most of us, but his amanuensis, Mr Mitchell, is clever. He decides how Simpy's lunacy can be directed. Mitchell is as cunning as a deputy heedie looking for promotion to the department of education itself, and that is cunning at that.

I happen to know that Mitchell is thinking far ahead to the day when Morris Simpson gets to be a headmaster or – as I have myself suggested in a previous Foreword – the Secretary of State in charge of education. But Mitchell is cunning. Even he knows that the Reichenbach Falls would kill more than his hero.

But Morris is no longer the only protagonist. *Chalk's Away!* has expanded the character of David Pickup to Homeric proportions. Pickup will now seriously enter the language of the school staffroom in the guise of the truly determined schoolteacher cynic. Pickup is dreadful of course, but he is the only hope for the future. Read this book and ponder and wonder. Wonder how Pickup came about. Ponder why.

All of these people in Mitchell's books are, despite his official disclaimers, based on real people; indeed Morris Simpson is based, a little unfairly really, on the author himself. Sometimes Mitchell is a bit cheeky and uses names which are almost identifiable. Almost.

But the realities are real enough. There really *are* teachers like Matthew Gordon who endow themselves with enough sick lines to wallpaper a social worker's suite of offices. There really *are* ghouls like pupil McLeary and they really are called Learie, and girls get called Rothesay and turn into ranting beasts. Ms Lelou exists. And so does Jack Ferguson who manages early retirement. Every level of madness which the gentle reader takes for exaggeration in this book is, believe me, all too true.

This book is about the surreal development in schools and, I may say, society at large. This book is bitter and sour, and no doubt about that. More bitter than the three preceding tomes. It is dark and devious the both. Devious because it is telling you the truth from the dank breath of the basement of education, but brightening you with laughter. Do not be misled by Mitchell's black humour. You might laugh, but you should greet instead.

I have come to admire Morris Simpson because he is there, despite it all. I know the meek will never inherit the earth. But Morris thinks they can, and I wish they can at that. It is, after all, what keeps most decent folk going.

Jack McLean, *The Herald*

From ***Advice to Young Teachers***, a paper prepared by – and reprinted by permission of – David Pickup, assistant principal teacher of religious education at Parkland Community High School:

'Upon leaving teacher-training college, you should choose the style and methodology of teaching which you intend to follow for the rest of your career. In subsequent years, and on many different occasions, you will be encouraged to alter that style and to amend that methodology, because new techniques will come into vogue. Yours may seem out of date. At all costs, resist the temptation to change it, because within ten years – or less – your style will be back in fashion once again, and you will then find yourself praised for being at the forefront of educational reform. The whole bloody thing just keeps going round in circles!'

Prologue

David Pickup – author of the advice to young teachers with which this volume has commenced – was a cynic, and happy to admit it. As a teacher of some twenty-eight years' standing he had seen fashions come. And he had seen fashions go.

Whether it be in the field of school organisation or of teaching methodologies, he was certain of one thing: today's educational bandwagon would be tomorrow's discredited theory. And tomorrow's discredited theory would – at some future point in time, when everyone had forgotten its manifold disadvantages – become yet another bandwagon, an educational epiphany attracting vast amounts of research money and implementation studies, possibly ruining the education of half a generation before it fell, once again, into disrepair.

Not everyone in Parkland Community High School thought that way, of course. Morris Simpson, in particular, maintained an optimistic willingness to embrace a multitudinous host of educational innovations in his unceasing attempt to impart knowledge unto youth, failing, as ever, to recognise that the impartation of knowledge is seldom a matter of priority in schools today. There are other, more important, things to be done.

Nevertheless, it was probably due to Simpson's continued and generally unquenchable enthusiasm for teaching that the editorial committee of the *Times Educational Supplement Scotland* decided to renew, at the beginning of his seventh year in teaching, Simpson's monthly contract for the reproduction of his increasingly chaotic school diaries. Although fully accepting that Simpson was a particularly unfortunate, even unrepresentative, example of a latter-day teacher, it was nevertheless felt that the ebullient optimism with which he reacted to his frequent misadventures would continue to act as a source of guidance, even inspiration, to young teachers who might find themselves similarly inconvenienced, or distressed, by the nature of their employment.

Readers who have already made the acquaintance of Morris Simpson will know that his style of teaching could be most kindly decribed as one of idealistic incompetence. Yet despite this incompetence – or, as David Pickup would say, *because* of it – by the end of his sixth year in teaching, Simpson had – almost – achieved a measure of promotion, to the post of assistant principal teacher (acting) of guidance.

As previous readers will also be aware, the uncertainty surrounding Simpson's near-elevation to APT status was due to an equivalent level of uncertainty surrounding the continued existence – or otherwise – of the school where he had spent his entire career to date. Indeed – according to David Pickup – Parkland Community High School was on its way out. He argued quite forcefully that, as the community which it professed to serve had long since disintegrated, then the school should consequently follow suit, and do so as quickly and as painlessly as possible.

In a sense, he was probably correct. It is no easy task teaching in a school like Parkland High even at the best of times, and it is particularly difficult when the threat of closure hangs over the establishment. Parents become worried about future prospects for their children, and will frequently choose to exercise their rights of removal to other, more populous centres of learning. A vicious circle develops, more pupils leave, and morale plummets.

It was for this reason, as much as any other, that Morris Simpson was not anticipating the new session with the same degree of enthusiasm as might normally be expected of the man. At the threshold of his seventh professorial year, he contined to reflect on the last days of the previous session, wherein he had discovered the marriage plans and pregnancy – although not in that order – of Fiona Strangelove, his attractive colleague from the English department, for whom Morris continued to harness a strong degree of affection himself. Alas, she had selected a less desirable soulmate in the person of Martin Pratt a pony-tailed history student who had been in school the previous session.

And then there was the constant round of petty staffroom arguments which, Simpson felt, diverted so much attention from the real task in hand: that of educating the children under his care. In this context, he thought particularly of Mr Ferguson and Mrs Leleu, whose job-sharing arrangement was, he felt certain, doomed to failure on the grounds of mutual dislike and diametrically opposed styles of teaching. Why on earth, he questioned himself, had the staffing department insisted upon such a dual placement when Ferguson had made clear his opposition to job-sharing with a French woman whom he had, in Morris's hearing, described as 'a little madam' and a 'jumped up firecracker'.

Mr Pickup had assured him that it was entirely *because* of

Ferguson's aggressive attitude and peremptory demands that the staffing department had exacted a particularly malicious revenge upon the man, but Morris refused to believe such a devious interpretation.

It was, then, with such ambivalent feelings and dubious forebodings for the forthcoming term that Morris Simpson boarded the early-morning bus on his way to Parkland that sunny August morning at the end of his summer holidays. As the Simpson diaries for the first week of term will reveal, his lowly expectations for the succeeeding five days were amply fulfilled.

August

Monday

A cloud of uncertainty hangs over Parkland Community High at the commencement of our new academic session.

To begin with, rumours of the school's possible merger with Rockston High had obviously circulated so effectively over the summer months that nearly 20% of our pupil roll had taken a unilateral decision to pre-empt any official announcement by requesting exceptional tranfers to other schools within the area, most notably to Rockston itself. It is all very demoralising for the staff, who long for nothing so much as a clear regional decision about our future, be it positive or negative.

My own near-promotion to acting APT guidance is still on hold because of all the uncertainty and – most unnerving of all – I have had to spend the six long weeks of summer planning a reaction to the first meeting of the term with my departmental colleague Fiona, erstwhile object of my desire but now unfortunately wedded to – and pre-maritally impregnated by – Martin Pratt, our bohemian history student of last session.

I couldn't help but think that it must have been terribly disappointing for the most important day of her life to have been soured by the awful necessity of the marriage arrangements, and thought it my place to lend a word of consolation. Heart aflutter, I took my courage in both hands and approached her rapidly-expanding figure at morning break.

'A brief word, Fiona?' I stammered.

'Sure, Morris!' she smiled happily. 'What can I do for you?'

'Just – uh – just a word of – uh, congratulation, really, Fiona,' I hesitated, '– on the – uh – happy event,' I motioned towards her stomach.

'Thanks, Morris! Much appreciated,' she nodded rosily, after which she pecked me on the cheek and started to turn away before I foolishly continued:

'And don't worry what anyone says about it all,' I tried to reassure her. 'Accidents *will* happen, and personally I don't think there's anything wrong about this sort of thing at all,' I confided, motioning once more towards her growing protruberance. 'Not nowadays ...' Unfortunately, my comfort and reassurance did not appear to be welcome, for her face suddenly froze.

'Nobody *has* said anything, Morris. And there *isn't* anything wrong about it, for your information. Everything that's happened this summer has been planned,' – my jaw dropped – 'in intimate and precise detail,' she concluded firmly, before tossing an imperious head and waddling angrily across the staffroom to share her incredulous annoyance with Monica Cunnungham.

I was only trying to be helpful.

Tuesday

My APT Gudance job's been confirmed! Richard Dick, our assistant head teacher, brought the news to me at morning break, just after Mr Tod had announced the region's decision on our potential merger. Apparently, the future of Parkland High is secure for at least another six months: there is to be a further period of consultation with assorted councillors and local pressure groups. A final (final) decision is to be taken after Christmas. Until then, the region has encouraged us to 'carry on as normal'.

'Bloody hell!' swore Mr Pickup 'Carry on as normal they say, with the sword of Damocles hanging over our ruddy heads! Why they can't just close this glorified toilet *now* and get it over and done with, is beyond me! If I had my way, then –'

I turned away to check Mr Dick's news again. 'So it's really true?' I asked excitedly. 'I'm to start acting up straight away?'

'Dead right, Morris. APT Guidance,' he confirmed. 'Look on it as a chance to give it all you've got, and join us in making Parkland Community High a school we can all be proud of!' – he glanced sharply at Mr Pickup – 'And if you need any help – at *any* time,' he assured me, 'just ask for it. And remember,' he emphasised, in Pickup's direction once again, 'we're all in there together, pitching and hitting for the good of the school.' With which exhortation he jabbed me sharply on the shoulder and confidently left the staffroom.

'In there together,' Pickup mimicked scornfully. 'Hah! In the shit, more like,' he muttered after the closing door. I began to protest, but Pickup wouldn't listen. 'If I've told you once, Morris, I've told you a thousand times: that little fart has got one interest, and one interest only – himself and his promotion prospects!'

'Mr Pickup!' I began again, but to no avail.

'All that balls about the good of the school! He couldn't give a monkey's about the school *or* the pupils! In fact, *especially* the pupils! The only anxiety in Dick Dick's mind at present is the short-leet selection for Freeman Secondary's depute headship.'

I explained my difference of opinion quite forcibly: to my mind, Mr Dick has shown a tremendous example of leadership since coming to Parkland, and I feel absolutely certain that he's already developed a strong loyalty to the school. 'And anyway,' I concluded, 'he's only been our assistant headteacher for a year now: he's hardly had time to settle in, never mind move on, Pickup!'

Pickup snorted and left the room. He's such an old cynic.

Wednesday

Mr Ferguson and Mrs Leleu are having difficulty in coming to terms with their job-sharing arrangement in the principal teacher of modern languages post. Their different styles of teaching have already led to a major disagreement during their changeover slot at lunchtime today, when Mr Ferguson arrived to commence his tour of duty for the next week.

I *had* understood that this fifty-minute session was intended to be a chance for them to update each other on the progress of different classes under their respective jurisdiction, and to suggest mutually agreeable solutions to any concerns or problems which had arisen with regard to any of the department's administrative procedures.

Instead, they spent the entire time shouting across the modern languages storecupboard at each other! Mr Ferguson, who has been perfectly happy using the same French course for the past fifteen years, had taken understandable umbrage at Mrs Leleu's somewhat premature decision to clear the storecupboard of a 'bunch of tatty old textbooks' in order to make room for her own, self-generated collection of desk-top published worksheets.

'So how the hell am I supposed to teach 2 G without any *books*, may I ask?' I overheard Jack Ferguson shouting as I walked past the storecupboard.

Francoise Leleu's attempted explanation to the effect that her own materials were infinitely superior to an outdated, uninspiring collection of grammar exercises was cut short, alas, by an unwholesome profanity from Mr Ferguson, after which exclamation he informed her that he was going to retrieve the aforementioned texts from the school dustbin whither they had been despatched by Mrs Leleu.

'And then,' he told her furiously, 'I can get on with some *real* teaching! Goodbye, Mrs Leleu. See you next Wednesday!'

I don't think this is quite the kind of co-operative educational venture which the region had in mind when it introduced job-sharing ...

Thursday

This guidance lark is beginning to look a bit more complex than I'd first imagined. To explain, I had some extremely irate parents at my office door this morning demanding to see their daughter's guidance teacher, Mr Parker.

My proud explanation that I was 'acting up' for Mr Parker did not seem to fill them with the reassurance I had hoped it would, but they eventually accepted my presence nevertheless, and explained the reason for their visit.

They seemed to think they had serious grounds for complaint because their daughter had been removed from the class of a French teacher whom they described as 'young, go-ahead, exciting and dynamic', and placed instead under the tutelage of an 'old-fashioned back-number in a gown who sucks peppermints all day.'

My attempts to explain the administrative procedures associated with, and the educational benefits to be derived from, the job-sharing agreement undertaken by Mrs Leleu and Mr Ferguson, were cut short by their sudden comprehension of the situation:

'You mean Samantha's going to have to put up with that old geezer every second week?' Mrs Knox demanded.

'Well, I can't –' I began to defend my elderly colleague, but her husband interrupted.

'And you mean Samantha's getting part-time teachers?' he thrust a belligerent fist on my desk. 'No way!'

My protestations were to no avail, as they expressed their joint intention of taking the matter to the highest authority in the school.

'I think you'll find the janitor's rather busy just now,' I tried to laugh the matter off, but they were in no mood for levity. We eventually agreed a compromise whereby I would investigate the possibility of Samantha changing French sections, and they went away mollified.

I was almost glad to get back to teaching English!

Friday

More guidance problems. Today's arose over lunchtime, when three other members of staff came into the staffroom and informed me that some of the third-year boys had been swearing and scuffling in the playground.

'Oh, thanks,' I said. 'Who were they?'

'Dunno,' said Simon Young. 'They're your guidance group, aren't they?'

'Well yes,' I admitted happily, 'but I can't record the incident if I don't know who was involved, now can I?'

'Well maybe you'd better *stop* the incident first, and *then* record it,' suggested Monica Cunningham.

'*What*?' I queried them. 'You mean you didn't break it up yourselves?'

'Nope,' Martin Henderson shrugged his shoulders carelessly. 'That's a guidance job, isn't it?'

His colleagues began to murmur in agreement as I jumped from my chair and scurried outside, just in time to witness Tommy McShane and Alan McLeary disappearing into a haze of dust, followed closely by several of their bedraggled classmates.

'Boys!' I shouted, but they obviously didn't hear me. Furious with my own colleagues, and mindful of Richard Dick's impassioned pleas to think of the school's reputation, I decided to take the matter to him in an effort to get a ruling on whole-school involvement with discipline. Surely, I thought, he would condemn the belief that staff could walk by on the other side on the ridiculous assertion that stopping playground brawls was a guidance matter.

To my distress, he was not as welcoming as I had hoped. Indeed, I got the distinct impression that he couldn't have cared less about my early difficulties in the guidance arena, and when I put it to him that I'd hoped he'd see his way to helping me – 'for the good of the school', as I reminded him – his eyes simply glazed over.

'Look, I'm sorry, Morris,' he shrugged his shoulders, 'but I'm really rather busy just now. Actually,' – and here he became suddenly animated, eyes alight with excitement – 'don't spread it about yet, will you – but I've got a hell of a lot of preparation to get on with –'

'Oh?' I queried, as he drew closer in confidence. 'What for?'

'Interview next month!' he whispered secretively. 'I'm on the shortleet for Freeman's depute!'

I gulped. 'Congratulations,' I eventually stammered out, but it was hard to take. So much for loyalty to the school!

September

Martin Henderson's refusal to assist Morris in the disciplinary misunderstanding at the end of August was hardly commendable. But it *was* understandable.

To explain, Martin had spent the previous two academic sessions as (acting) principal teacher of history, while Sandra Denver, who was Parkland's (principal) principal teacher of history was absent on successive bouts of maternity leave, both of them admirably timed to ensure that her return to active service (and full pay) would coincide with the onset of the summer holidays. Martin, meanwhile, having peformed her job for the duration of both academic sessions had nevertheless found himself reduced to standard pay for two successive summer holidays.

At least, this term, he had reckoned that Miss Denver would be unlikely to demonstrate sufficient fecundity to announce a *third* pregnancy, and in this assumption he had been proved correct. Alas for Martin, however, some three weeks subsequent to her return from holiday Sandra Denver had been awarded the post of history staff development officer on a two-year secondment to the regional offices, and thus it was that Henderson found himself once again *in situ* as (acting) principal teacher for the third year in a row, without having received any of the accompanying financial benefits throughout the summer break.

It all seemed most unfair to him, and it was therefore with some sympathy that Morris discovered Henderson's reasons for refusing to perform any pedagogical services which were not strictly within the bounds of his contract. The same excuse could not be made, of course, for Monica Cunningham and George Crumley in refusing to help break up the playground fight, but their apparent lack of professional responsibility should really have been nothing new to Morris, and it was a mark of his continuing idealism that he affected such surprise at their response.

Of even greater shock to him, of course, was the reaction of Richard Dick, the assistant head who had helped Morris in his quest for promotion the previous term. He had thought to have found himself a real friend in Richard Dick, and refused to believe Mr Pickup's repeated – and accurate – assertions that Dick's assistance had been based purely on the grounds of self-interest, the full narrative of which motivation was outlined in *Absolutely Chalked Off!*, the volume of Simpson's pedagogical memories immediately preceding this one.

For the moment, suffice to say that promotion seekers such as Richard Dick tend to have little genuine interest in people other than themselves, as Mr Pickup was to point out forcibly to Morris at the end of September. Also of note in this month's entry were the new style of national Higher examinations recently introduced to home economics, wherein Simpson's concern is evident over the problems which had arisen in ensuring uniformity of marking standards across the country, not to mention his surprise upon discovering the somewhat flawed nature of the examination itself.

With only 22 passes out of 580 candidates, it would indeed appear to have been flawed.

And, of course, the school was still under threat of closure, a continued source of motivational distress for parents and staff alike. To Mr Pickup, the solution was simple.

Monday

More pupils are leaving Parkland High with every passing day, as the regional authority continues to vacillate over the future of the school. Meanwhile, our list of requests for exceptional transfers continues to grow.

'Honest to God,' exclaimed Mr Pickup as he scanned the latest newspapers this morning. 'They're providing sixteen different options for future educational provision within Parkland district when any half-witted councillor worth the courage of his own convictions would come down like a ton of bricks and transfer the lot of us to Rockston High before the month's out! After which,' he added in bitter conclusion, 'they could raze this place to the ground before one of our former pupils decides to do the job for them!'

I thought he was still being rather premature, and told him that the Headmaster had only this morning sent out a letter to all parents assuring them that – despite a pupil roll which has now fallen below 350 – he was entirely confident of the school's continued viability into the next session and beyond, and urging them to cease the alarming haemorrhage of transfers.

'Hah!' barked Pickup in return. 'That settles it! If Johnny Ross says we're staying open, then we're obviously for the chop! Talk about sticking his finger in a dyke!'

I excused myself from further fruitless discussion by pleading business in my guidance office, where I was due to meet up with some errant pupils and their respective punishment exercises. I have now waited nearly four weeks for the essays concerned ('Why I Must Not Fight In The Playground') from Alan McLeary and Tommy McShane, and was infuriated to discover their continued non-appearance when I went to meet up with them. If they don't produce the work soon, I'm going to have to take some drastic action!

Tuesday

More guidance difficulties with the parents of Samantha Knox:

they are still distressed by the contrasting teaching styles of their daughter's job-sharing French teachers, and have initiated a block request by every like-minded parent with pupils in the same class (i.e. all of them) to be transferred to another French section; otherwise, they threaten, a similarly corporate request will be made to the regional authorities for a 21-strong transfer of their respective offspring to Rockston High!

'It's no good, Morris,' Richard Dick was extremely blunt when I took the problem to him this afternoon. 'They've got you by the short and curlies, I'd say – and if Mr Ross discovers that the sudden decimation of his third year is down to your inability to smoothe the waters on this one, then I'd say your chances of retaining a permanent guidance post might begin to look pretty slim. Get Jack Ferguson to change the sections, can't you?'

'Well, it's a bit embarrassing if he's the one they all hate – and it's hardly my fault if Mr Ferguson's such an appalling teacher and Mrs Leleu's –'

'The privilege of promotion, my boy,' he tried to calm me with a few fatherly words of advice – a bit of a cheek considering he's younger than I am, but well-intentioned nonetheless. 'It can be tough at the top,' he continued, 'and even tougher getting there ...'

Which reminded me – as it was no doubt meant to – that Dick's due at interview tomorrow for Freeman Secondary's depute head post, a job in which he has every confidence of finding himself by the end of term.

'How *are* the interview preparations, then?' I made the enquiry so obviously expected of me.

'All done, Morris,' he was happy to inform me before unearthing a voluminous collection of folders containing lengthy and detailed reports of all the projects which he has initiated and co-ordinated since coming to Parkland: Records of Achievement; Special Needs Provision in a Multi-Cultural Framework; a Staff Appraisal Scheme; Adult Remediation Strategies in English and Computer Related Assistance in Pastoral Suppport, to name but five of them – the collection seemed endless.

Indeed, so enthusiastic did he become in his narration of the first answer he was planning to give at the interview tomorrow – a remarkable feat of prescience considering he could hardly know the question – that I completely forgot to ask his advice about the ill-behaved louts on my guidance group who have still to produce their punishment exercises. I think I'm going to have to get tough with them.

Wednesday

A bewildering report from Miss Tarbet of home economics this morning, to the effect that she had just been contacted by the examination board with a view to placing an appeal for her solitary higher candidate last session. Apparently, the board has been distressed at the abnormally low national pass-rate in her subject's higher grade examination (22 candidates out of 580) and is now engaged in a frantic bout of telephone calls to principal teachers urging appeals for all but the semi-literate.

'But that's just the point!' Miss Tarbet explained to us at morning break. 'Amanda Watson's completely *sub*-literate! She can hardly write her own name, never mind finish an exam paper! The girl only scored 5% for her prelim and the board's wanting me to appeal for her!'

'Didn't you tell them that?' enquired Monica Cunningham.

'Of course I did! But the guy assured me it was worth the girl's while all the same, and they'd be looking extremely kindly upon any positive evidence that might suggest she *would* have passed – if only,' – she added herself – '*they'd* managed to present an examination paper in the first place which bore even passing resemblance to their own ruddy syllabus!'

'So what are you doing?'

'Appealing for her – may as well, if you ask me.'

I shook my head quietly and sought out Mr Pickup for his view on the matter, but he was too busy anticipating – with some relish, I might add – the imminent departure of Mr Dick. Again, I feel he is being somewhat premature in anticipating a successful outcome for our assistant head's promotion lunge, but he seemed certain of the likely conclusion:

'Look, Simpson: I've said since Day One of that little oink's arrival here that he'd be sucking himself further up the greasy pole before you could say Brylcreem – and so it's proved. He's never had an interview in his *life* that he hasn't oozed himself through by dint of highlighting his overwhelming enthusiasm for management training and curricular initiatives – and his overwhelming dislike of actually teaching children! He's had more new jobs than he's had new shoes, and he's never been in one post long enough to get found out for the charlatan he is – and the only people who discover *that* are the simpletons like us who're left behind to clear up the appalling messes he leaves behind him. The sooner he goes, Simpson, the better, and then we can all get back to leading a quiet life in here. He's destined for the very top, Morris, you mark my words. And they bloody well deserve him!' He stopped to draw breath long enough for me to get a word in edgeways and pass on the gossip that's sweeping the staffroom at the moment about Mr Carswell, recently re-elected as chairman of the school board for a third session of somewhat dubious legality.

'He's supposed to be planning a campaign to save the school,' I tried to divert Pickup from his misanthropic complaints about Richard Dick, and the news certainly had an effect – of sorts:

'Oh my God!' Pickup wailed into his coffee cup. 'Not *another* one,' he recalled our last such campaign over two years ago.

'Afraid so,' I confirmed. 'And I gather he's planning for an opt-out ballot as well.'

'You what!' Pickup nearly fell off his chair with laughter. 'Half of the parents here couldn't even *read* a ballot paper, let alone turn up on the right day to vote in one! Oh well,' he relaxed once more. 'If that's all he's got up his sleeve, then I think we can all rest safely in our beds – and get the window-shutters out in time for Christmas.'

I wonder if he underestimates Mr Carswell.

Thursday

Mr Dick didn't get the job! Nobody's managed to get the full story yet – Dick rang in sick at ten to nine this morning – but his whole world must have collapsed around him. Imagine! His first failed interview at twenty-nine years of age!

Mr Pickup was torn between outright glee at (in his own words) 'such a well-deserved come-uppance for the cocky little bastard' on the one hand, and a good degree of bewilderment on the other, mainly at the erroneous nature of his own prediction concerning Dick's rose-strewn promotion path.

'I can't understand it,' he confided in me at morning break. 'I thought he had it all sewn up. Unless,' he mused aloud, '– unless he's crossed swords with a dodgy councillor ...'

'Sorry?'

'Unless he's ...' he tailed off in thought once more. 'I know!' he slapped a fist into his palm: 'I'll 'phone up Davie Samson and get the low-down on the interview!'

Further enquiry revealed that Pickup has a councillor friend on the education committee who is likely to have inside information on the procedures pertaining to yesterday's appointment of a new depute for Freeman Secondary. He has promised to keep me in touch.

Of more immediate concern to me, however, was the fact that Alan McLeary and Tommy McShane have *still* to hand in their month-old punishment exercises. I have written a letter to the parents of both boys outlining the problems I have had in disciplining their wayward children, and have told them that I expect to see the boys at my office tomorrow morning with the punishments completed. It seems ridiculous that one has to enlist parental authority to support the discipline of the school, but that seems to be more necessary than ever in the current educational climate.

Changed days it is.

Friday

Changed days indeed! Far from supporting the disciplinary attempts of their children's overworked guidance team, Messrs McLeary and McShane have seen fit to flaunt the school's authority in the most flagrantly disrespectful manner.

'Well, boys?' I had enquired of my budding pugilists at 9 o'clock this morning. 'Where are your punishments?'

'Ah've no' done it,' drawled McLeary.

'Me neither!' confirmed McShane. 'Ma dad says ah've no' to dae it.'

'Mine too!' triumphed McLeary. 'Says ah wisny fightin', an' if ye want tae give punny eccies, then see him furst aboot it. An' if ye don't, ye can stuff it! Sur!'

I have always been unnerved by the fact that a boy such as McLeary can make the term 'Sir' a marker of flagrant disrespect rather than appropriate obeisance, but I was too amazed by the sudden turn of events to consider this particular breach of etiquette. Unable to frame a suitable reply, I dismissed them from my presence forthwith and went in search of Richard Dick for some words of advice. Unfortunately, he is still suffering from shock, and had locked himself into his room for the duration of the entire day, as it later transpired.

'It's just as well that he doesn't have to teach many classes,' I remarked to Mr Pickup at lunchtime, before asking whether he'd been able to get the low-down on Wednesday's job interview yet.

'Tchah!' he threw his head back in frustration. 'Not quite. Telephoned Davie Samson last night, but he was just about to leave for the airport.'

'Oh?'

'Yeh – he and fourteen other councillors are away for an all-expenses paid fact-finding mission with our twin-town brethren in Austria: going to investigate their new theme-park leisure facilities over there – and a few five-star restaurants as well, I shouldn't wonder,' he said scornfully.

I made comment upon the disgraceful waste of public money occasioned by such a junket, but Pickup was keener to tell me that Mr Samson has promised a session at The Pig and Whistle upon his return from Austria, complete with every intimate detail of Richard Dick's failed job interview, and a pledge to make Pickup's hair – if he had any, that is – stand on end with the hilarity of the day's events. I can hardly wait ...

October

As the power of school boards in educational affairs has increased, so the influence of local councillors upon the selection of promoted posts in schools is less than it used to be. Gone, one hopes, are the days of a semi-literate selection committee whose most piercing question of a headship candidate would concern a verification of the number of Highers possessed by the applicant.

Nevertheless, there were still a goodly number of councillors who viwed the educational profession with mistrust, and it was unfortunate for Richard Dick that one such locally elected member, Councillor Bill Malcolm, had an all-consuming suspicion of the educational jargon by which Mr Dick set such store. Also, Mr Malcolm had heard a number of rumours concerning the pilot appraisal scheme set up by Mr Dick the previous term, and was keen to question his judgement in awarding a glowing testimonial to the only teacher willing to assist him in the pilot scheme, a certain Mr Morris Simpson. Never one to call a spade anything other than a spade, Councillor Malcolm made it his bounden duty to get straight to the heart of things, as the record of Dick's failed interview which appeared in October's diary will confirm.

Also in that month, it is interesting to note the launch of Alan Carswell's second opt-out campaign for the school. It was a campaign which owed more to Carswell's plans for self-determination and realignment of educational opportunity within Parkland High rather than for any continuation of the *staus quo* and, as such, was unlikely to win the support of many regionally-employed staff. Except, perhaps, Mr Pickup.

For Morris, however, greater concern was still felt over his guidance involvement in the row over the French department's job-sharing controversy. It was certainly clear to Morris that Francoise Leleu, fresh from her own secondment in developing innovative teaching materials for the region, had a more lively and interesting approach than Jack Ferguson. Unfortunately, Mr Ferguson didn't see it quite like that.

Monday

I am still experiencing severe problems over the matter of the school's job-sharing principal teachers of modern languages. Their diametrically opposed styles of teaching have led to continued complaints from the parents of my guidance year-group, most especially about the more traditional approaches to language teaching undertaken by Mr Ferguson compared with the youthful dynamism displayed by Mrs Leleu.

Unfortunately, any tactful attempts to remedy the situation in my guidance office this morning rather backfired; Jack Ferguson seemed to misunderstand my request for an alteration in class arrangements to assuage parental discontent over the differing pedagogical philosophies expressed by himself and his job-sharer:

'Hah!' he barked triumphantly. 'So *they're* fed up with Francoise Leleu as well, are they? Wondered how long it would take before they'd see through that bloody woman and her fancy notions. Honest to God, Simpson! Puzzles, word-searches, colouring-in grids – and none of them a bit of good in teaching the little buggers some French! The woman seems to think they'll learn to speak the lingo by some kind of osmosis – the only time they actually get any proper *teaching* done is when I'm looking after them – and then I've got to spend half the week undoing all the havoc *she's* created while I've been away!'

'Well, actually, Mr Ferguson –' I tried to explain the awkwardness of my situation, but it was no use.

'Awkward, Simpson? Not at all! It's about time somebody told that woman some home truths about the educational chaos she's created with her modern methods. I'll get the classes rearranged, don't you worry – and tell Samantha Knox's mum and dad that I plan to start taking 3B for all of their French timetable as soon as possible, and that they'll be getting down to some good old-fashioned grammar for a change.'

'But it's the other –' I started to protest, but to no avail.

'Don't you worry about it, Simpson,' he assured me once more. 'In a way, I'm glad it's come to a head like this. Good to get it out in the open, don't you think?' With which rhetorical question he waved a confident hand in the air, left my office and shut the door behind him.

I recall being told that guidance is all about tact, discretion and courtesy: that would be fine if all I had to deal with were obtuse *children* ...

Tuesday

'Remembering Thursday night, Morris?' Mr Pickup greeted me at morning break today.

'Sorry?' I queried.

'Thursday night. The Pig and Whistle – for the low-down on Dick Dick's failed interview last month.'

'Gosh, yes!' I recalled the appointment with Pickup's councillor friend. 'Is David Samson back from his exchange visit then?'

'Yup! Twenty-four days of endless free bevvy from his twin-town councillor brethren in Kotzburg, just so they can borrow their architect's plans for a new swimming pool. Why the hell they couldn't fax the bloody things over, God only knows! Still, Davie's promised a few entertaining revelations about our smarmy little friend's most recent attempts to –'

'Weeshht!' I cautioned him as Mr Dick scurried into the staffroom – folder in hand – and consulted his pigeon hole. Empty. Whereupon he scurried out again.

'He seems to have recovered his poise slightly,' I commented to Pickup, recalling Mr Dick's initially incredulous reaction to his unsuccessful interview for a depute-head's post. 'He was just telling me yesterday that he'd never really wanted the depute's job at Freeman, but he'd gone in for it so as to get some interview experience.'

'Bollocks' jeered Pickup scornfully. 'Interviewing's the only thing he *has* got any experience of. He certainly hasn't got much in teaching, I'll tell you that!'

Sometimes I almost feel sorry for Richard Dick – cynics like Pickup must make it very dificult to keep one's educational faith intact.

Wednesday

Mr Carswell's plans to hold an opt-out ballot to prevent the closure of Parkland High have been gathering momentum – we have just heard that our school board chairman has proclaimed himself leader of a campaign based on every child's right to what he terms a 'Basic Evangelical Education', as outlined in the opting-out petition which was circulating the staffroom this morning. It appears to be a high-risk ballot strategy, because his suggested remediation for an opted-out school seems intent upon abandoning the region's innovative curricular policies which are aimed at increasing equal opportunities for all ethnic groups. In short, Carswell demands a return to a curriculum aimed at the interests of what he quaintly describes as 'the longer-term generational residents of Parkland district'. Unsurprisingly, Pickup declared himself in full agreement as he scanned the literature.

'Bang on!' he stamped a fist on the table and lifted his eyes from Carswell's manifesto 'You know, for once I agree with the man,' he jabbed a finger at the document. 'For too long now, this place's been catering for every ruddy minority under the sun. Except us!'

'Pardon?' I queried.

'Except us! White Anglo-Saxon Protestants, my boy! Look at the ruddy torrent of policy documents that come in on teaching in Urdu and Punjabi and Gujurati – does anyone teach English any more? Not bloody likely! They're all too busy pandering to the loud-mouthed yobs with their snouts in the multi-cultural trough of money. And all that Alan Carswell's asking for is a return to basic –'

'*Excuse* me, Mr Pickup,' Fiona Pratt glared fiercely at Pickup from across the staffroom. 'You don't mean to tell me you actually *support* the appalling racism contained in this –'

'It's hardly racism, my dear,' patronised Pickup. 'Just good old common sense, and –'

'My God!' Fiona held her hand to her brow. 'He's actually serious,' she gazed disbelievingly at Monica Cunningham, who nodded in sympathetic agreement. 'I'm only too glad I'm going off soon,' she announced angrily, in a reference to her impending maternity leave, '– at least I won't have to listen to crap like this for much longer.'

'Listen, dearie –' started Pickup once more, but I had had enough. I pursed my lips and left the staffroom. It was hardly what you would call a professional discussion ...

Thursday

An entertaining diversion in The Pig and Whistle this evening, wherein Councillor Samson outlined just what had come to pass behind the closed doors of Richard Dick's failed interview last month. Word had spread about the likely discussion topic for the evening, with the result that a goodly proportion of Parkland Community High School's teaching complement found itself gathered around Mr Samson's revelatory bar-stool.

Apparently, Dick had started the interview with the full support of both educationists on the panel (a divisional officer and the head teacher of Freeman secondary), but his opening eulogy upon 'articulation of modules within the senior school' had drawn the suspicious eye of Councillor Malcolm, a man whose knowledge of education is apparently limited to a two-year sabbatical stint as president of his student union.

'And presumably that's why he was picked for the education panel?' queried Pickup. 'Knows sod all about it?'

'Mmm,' confirmed Samson. 'Anyway, things got worse when Dick started wittering on about moderation of internal assessment and then, so help me, outlined his views on differentiation within the curriculum.

'Pardon?' says Bill Malcolm. 'What's differentiation when it's at home?'

'Well, um,' says Dick. 'It's, um – differentiation. It's – uh – what lets you differentiate between … uh …'

'The bugger didn't know!' exclaimed David Samson. 'Wittered on for five minutes, but couldn't give a definition in plain English of differentiation – or of any other piece of educational jargon that he kept spouting out either, come to that.

'Things went from bad to worse when he tried to give a glowing self-promotional job about his Records of Achievement scheme that he's started up at your place – three breathless minutes on the educational nirvana to be achieved by all schools who took up similar schemes, then Malcolm hits him with a steely glare and says:

'Records of Achievement, Mr Dick? D'you mean *report cards*? From your description of them to me just now, that's what Records of Achievment would seem to be. Tarted up report cards!'

A gale of laughter erupted around Councillor Samson as he gladly accepted another drink from his excited audience and continued with his sorry tale. Alas, for Richard Dick, the next topic to come up had apparently been that of school closures. Thinking to win himself several brownie points, he had foolishly chosen to commend the region's school closure plans, with particular reference to the economic and educational benefits to be obtained from closing Parkland High whilst retaining one of our neighbouring schools, St Ainsley's. And all, alas, blissfully unaware of Councillor Malcolm's close personal and democratic interest in the continued survival of Parkland High (his is a marginal seat, apparently) and the longed-for closure of St Ainsley's, whose minority denominational interests are not those closest to his heart (he is a rabid Protestant, apparently).

Dick's next indignity – having further related the list of wondrous educational initiatives at Parkland for which he claimed responsibility – had been a fearsome googly from Councillor Malcolm about some of Parkland's favoured pupils, particularly those whom Malcolm named and who are currently enjoying limited success at the region's arts festival. Unhappily, Mr Dick had never heard of them, and it soon became apparent that he was completely unable to name any pupil whatsoever in the school!

'Of course not,' interrupted Mr Pickup. 'He knows everything about education. And nothing about children!'

'Mmm,' agreed David Samson again. 'Anyway, he ended up babbling about some appraisal scheme he'd tried to start up at Parkland, and Malcolm said that, yes, he'd heard all about the glowing report he'd given to some incompetent half-wit on your staff who couldn't teach his way out of a paper bag!' I blushed furiously and hoped nobody else would recognise the reference, although – from the assorted sniggers and nudgings it seemed that quite a lot of people did. 'And that just about finished him off,' concluded David Samson, '– walked out of the interview like a headless chicken, muttering about policy documents and interdisciplinary liaison before letting out the most enormous wail as he closed the door behind him. And that was the end of that.'

'Good!' adjudged Pickup. 'Serve the little fart right! Thanks for the entertainment, Davie – another drink?'

'Yes please,' replied Samson. 'And tell me – was that right about the rose-coloured appraisal he gave out for the doughball?'

I interrupted swiftly with the observation that he must have been mistaken, as Parkland High's appraisal scheme has yet to be properly validated. Several members of staff seemed to be simultaneously overtaken by severe fits of choking, but at least Pickup had the decency to back me up. Sometimes he's not such a bad old stick after all.

Friday

Back to earth with a bump after last night's hilarity. Mr Tod, our depute head, told me this afternoon that Francoise Leleu was 'on the warpath'. She had apparently been in receipt of a letter from Jack Ferguson (they stopped talking to each other three weeks ago) which had made a unilateral declaration of his authority by reallocating class lists so that he took over the entire responsibility for teaching 3 B as well as both certificate classes in the languages department.

Mrs Leleu wants a meeting with me, as Ferguson had informed her that the new arrangememts were being made as a result of a confidential complaint from one of the guidance staff about her methods of teaching.

'Hmm,' sympathised Pickup when I told him of my plight. 'Showdown at the Champs Elysées by the sound of it, Morris. What is it you keep saying about guidance work? Based on tact, courtesy and discretion, isn't it?'

'Indeed,' I nodded in assent. 'Especially discretion.' He nodded back, raised his eyebrows – and we left for the pub.

November

Although Morris was not to know it at the time, the difficulties surrounding the job-share between Mr Ferguson and Mrs Leleu were soon to be resolved. It would be pleasant to report that the solution was arrived at by the means of tactful, discrete and courteous discussion between all parties, but in truth the conflict was ended by the imposition of external circumstances, as will be discovered in the Simpson diaries for November of that year.

It was as well that such internal disputes were removed from the Simpson worry-list, because another guidance problem asserted itself in that month: the case of Rothesay O'Brien. Morris had thought that the girl's attention-seeking behaviour had calmed down of late, an improvement which he attributed to the slight improvement in the stability of her home circumstances over the previous six months, as well as to the careful counselling and positive reinforcement which he had lavished upon the girl. Unfortunately, not all of the staff at Parkland High were as sympathetic as Morris, and Mr Dunbar of maths proved more unsympathetic than most.

But this is to anticipate, if only slightly. Simpson's initial concern, at the end of November, remained the impasse between Mr Ferguson and Mrs Leleu. And he had decided to do something about it.

Monday

I have taken the initiative of arranging a meeting tomorrow between Mr Ferguson, Mrs Leleu and myself. The aim of our tripartite discussion is to arrive at an amicable solution over the continuing disagreements regarding their job-share. I am given little cause for hope by Mrs Leleu's announced intention to 'seurt eout that leetle old besket once and feur all' at the meeting in question.

I told Mr Pickup that I was rather concerned about her volatile Gallic temperament, but he told me that such a comment was racist and offensive before snorting into his coffee cup.

'You *wanted* the guidance job, Morris,' he chortled, 'and you'll just have to accept everything that goes with it.'

'I hardly think that *you're* qualified to criticise anyone on racist grounds, Mr Pickup,' I rejoined. 'Not after your ridiculous support for Mr Carswell's opt-out campaign.'

That hit home. He refused to comment, turned away in his seat, and fell to whistling a tuneless version of *Land of Hope and Glory*. I have to say that I've been appalled at the way in which Pickup has been the only staff member not to speak out against our school board chairman's attempts to proclaim Parkland Community High as a school under imminent threat of takeover by ethnic minority interests. Carswell's campaign for an opted-out school providing a Basic Evangelical Education (pathetically labelled a 'BEES for WASPS Initiative' by Pickup) looks doomed to failure. He has the support of nobody except Pickup on the staff, and only about 10% of the parents, most of whom seem perfectly happy with the multilateral support given by the region to all ethnic groupings. It seems doubtful, however, whether Carswell will concede defeat. It is not a word in the zealot's vocabulary ...

Tuesday

A strangely inconclusive meeting with our job-sharing principal teachers of modern languages this morning. I had expected fireworks, and tried to calm matters down beforehand by utilising the stress-counselling techniques I have been learning on my guidance courses.

It all seemed pointless, to be honest. I outlined some relaxation exercises I wanted them both to practise before we started talking, but Mrs Leleu sat fizzing angrily while Mr Ferguson simply gazed vacantly into space.

'Oh, cut eet out, Mister Seempson,' she eventually broke in angrily. 'Wee aven't got the time for stroking each other's temples, even if wee ad the incleenation,' – and here she glanced sharply at Ferguson before launching into an impassioned diatribe about the completely discredited, outdated and even antiquated teaching methods employed by her 'euther half', and explaining that if I really wanted to sort out the problems of my third year guidance group – not to mention the complaints of their parents – then the first thing she advised me to do was to file a grievance complaint against the appalling lack of professionalism displayed by Jack Ferguson, whom she went on to decribe as a 'part-time teecher, and feull-time leauffer!'.

'Leauffer?' I queried, desperately interrupting to play for time and halt the inevitable outburst from Ferguson.

'Yes, leauffer!' she declared, before sitting back in her chair, folding her arms, and daring Ferguson to contradict her.

I waited for the response. To my amazement, the man seemed completely unconcerned. Relaxing in his chair, he simply gazed into space for a further half-minute, after which cogitative diversion he sat up straight, raised two fingers at his opposite number and blew an extremely loud raspberry. After which he strode purposefully out of the room.

It was hardly a positive contribution to the discussion.

Wednesday

Tried to seek out Mr Dick for his advice on Mr Ferguson and Mrs Leleu, but our dynamic assistant head was nowhere to be found. Mr Crumley of geography informed me between gritted teeth that Dick was 'out on another ruddy course: active listening, for God's sake!' This was a new one on me, but Crumley didn't seem predisposed to explain the precise nature of the course, choosing instead to describe it as 'another chance for the wee slimebag to escape from the kids for a couple of days.' It hardly seemed a professional assessment of his colleague's curricular motives, but I left it at that.

Even Mr Pickup, at break, seemed unable to explain the benefits of an active listening course, other than to agree with Crumley's assessment of it as a temporary bolt-hole for a child-phobic teacher.

'No doubt it'll all become clear when he gets back,' Pickup ruminated. 'He'll have us all on active listening duty for the next three weeks until he's off on his next furlough. What did you want him for anyway, Morris?'

I started to describe Mr Ferguson's gross rudeness towards Mrs Leleu yesterday afternoon, but was interrupted before I could finish.

'But haven't you heard?' Pickup broke in. 'Ferguson's cracked it at last!'

'Cracked what?'

'His early retirement! His escape tunnel's come up on the other side and he's hanging up his duster on Friday!'

'Friday?' I queried. 'As quickly as that?'

'Yeh. Staffing 'phoned up on Monday and made him an offer he couldn't refuse as long as he cleared out within the week.'

'Really?'

'Yeh. Well – actually it was more of an offer he couldn't *understand*, to be honest. Have *you* ever tried to work out twenty-four thirty-eighths of your annual salary plus a farewell lump sum minus a few incremental allowances? Poor bugger was in here with a calculator all Monday afternoon trying to work out what he'd get in his greedy little paws if he accepted the offer –'

'So *that's* why 3B were left unattended for their French lesson?' I explained the complaints of Mr and Mrs Knox which had reached my ears only this morning. Pickup confirmed the likelihood of my assessment before asking for a contribution to Ferguson's going-away presentation on Friday afternoon.

I searched my pockets for whatever loose change I could come up with, but could only find a pound coin, for which meagre sum I apologised to Pickup. He pursed his lips, narrowed his eyes, and announced that it approximated to 'roughly three pence for every year of Jack's teaching career – and given his contribution to education, Simpson, I'd reckon that's more than generous! It's certainly more than anyone *else* has given – only got enough for a decent bottle of sherry so far, and I'm half-way round the staff already!'

Fancy. And after all of Mr Ferguson's hard years of toil.

Thursday

More trouble with the third year. This time it's Rothesay O'Brien, my attention-seeking adolescent with a severe behavioural maladjustment condition – at least that's what her educational psychologist called it.

I *had* thought the girl to have calmed down dramatically in the last six months, but all of her old problems appear to be surfacing once more: the nose-bleeds she can produce at will and the head-banging off her desk, not to mention the regularity with which she can continue to bite her own arm until it bleeds.

'So what are you going to do about it, Simpson?' demanded Mr Dunbar of me this morning. 'It's very difficult to do quadratic equations with that little bitch spraying blood all over the desk and thumping her head up and down off it half the time.'

'Mr Dunbar!' I chastised him. 'That's hardly a very sympathetic approach, you know.'

'Sod the sympathy!' he thrust back at me. '*My* sympathy's with the twenty-two other kids in her class who can't get a stroke of work done for all the havoc created by *that* one. And *you're* her guidance teacher, Simpson. So what are you going to *do* about it?'

It was difficult to know what to say. My professionalism wouldn't allow me to reveal that Rothesay's home life is currently undergoing yet another dramatic upheaval, as her present step-father (Mr O'Brien) is in the process of being replaced in her mother's affections by yet another 'uncle', a Mr Anthony Kyle (or 'big Tony', as Rothesay is wont to affectionately describe him). Sadly, the domestic shenanigans pertaining to the new romance in Mrs O'Brien's life are understandably having an adverse effect on her daughter's academic attainments: hence the return to the old pattern. But I couldn't tell Dunbar all this.

'I'll see what I can do, Mark,' I tried to placate him. 'I'll have a quiet word with Rothesay as soon as I can.'

'Hmmph,' he scoffed. 'It's more than a quiet word she needs, in my opinion.' He paused. 'But *you're* her guidance teacher, Simpson. I'll leave it with you.'

Suddenly it seems as if I am to be held personally responsible for the behaviour of Rothesay O'Brien: it hardly seems fair …

Friday

Disgraceful news from the examination board this morning: Miss Tarbet of home economics was still shaking her head with incredulity just before Jack Ferguson's presentation this afternoon.

'Imagine!' she proclaimed to the assembled company before the official proceedings got underway. 'Amanda Stewart can hardly write her own name, yet she comes away with a B Grade in her appeal for the home economics Higher – and all because their first exam was too hard for a PhD so they start awarding marks to any monkey who requests a second shot! Look at these examiner's comments,' she complained, brandishing a document around the coffee table. 'They say it was because of her "exceptionally innovative personal study" – God save us! – "that they've overlooked some of the other irregularities in her answer paper" – like she can't write – "to make the award".'

'And what was her personal study?' queried Fiona Pratt.

'Baked beans!' Miss Tarbet shook her head. 'Baked bloody beans! And she gets a B Grade! Still, who am I to complain? Bumped up the pass rate by a hundred per cent …'

Is it any wonder that employers view our examination standards with suspicion when such appalling machinations are going on behind their backs?

Meanwhile, Mr Pickup was having some difficulty in getting Jack Ferguson's presentation off the ground: he had apparently spent a good twenty minutes before the interval trying to sober up our retiring colleage after their lunchtime excesses at The Pig and Whistle, but to little avail. Fortunately, Mr Ross was able to instruct the janitor to extend the interval slightly while they tried to get Ferguson out of the toilet, so in the meantime I was able to seek out the freshly-returned Richard Dick for some advice about Rothesay O'Brien.

It was a slightly unnerving encounter, to be honest. Mr Dick kept staring deeply into my eyes as I spoke, nodding all the while, and muttering 'Yes, Yes,' and 'I know, I know,' at practically every word I uttered about poor Rothesay. It really did seem as if he was listening closely to what I was saying for once, though I was left to ponder the accuracy of this assessment as he laid a hand on my forearm after I had finished pouring out my woes:

'Fine, Morris,' he encouraged me. 'That's just fine. Pleased to hear about it. Let me know how you get on with that one, won't you? Better stop now. The presentation's about to start.'

And so it was. My doubts about Dick's perception of my difficulties were swiftly forgotten as I witnessed the unforgettable sight of Jack Ferguson – his tie seriously adrift – lurching dangerously across the staffroom and staggering into his favourite corner armchair, there to fall into apparent unconsciousness while Mr Ross paid him the tribute of a 45-second peroration outlining his professed sadness at Ferguson's departure from the staff.

Fortunately, Ferguson seemed to choke slightly on some phlegm in his throat, for his ensuing coughing fit woke him up sufficiently to make what amounted to his valedictory speech of reply.

In it, he mumbled some thanks to Mr Ross for the cheque he had just received which – he announced after examining the figures – would allow him to buy 'one exshtra round in The Pig and Whishtle after school. Thanksh for your generoshity,' he slurred bitterly in ill-conceled sarcasm. Thereafter, he placed on record his further and immense gratitude to the divisional education officer for the letter of congratulations he had sent upon Ferguson's retirement after 28 years of loyal service: it was, he claimed, only *slightly* less personal than a Reader's Digest circular, and he looked forward to having it framed in the toilet of his villa in the south of France, where he looked forward to spending his declining years.

'And thatsh about ash far away from thish bloody toilet of a school ash I'm able to get!' he slurred again. 'Cheersh!' With which he collapsed once more into his armchair and fell quietly asleep.

It was all most embarrassing – and a somewhat anti-climactic conclusion, I'd have to admit, to a career of such outstanding educational merit as Jack Ferguson's. May he rest in peace.

December

Jack Ferguson was not missed from Parkland Community High School, it has to be admitted. The man had grown bitter, jaded, and stale in his teaching, and his departure certainly allowed Morris to concentrate on the guidance problems for which he was supposed to be responsible: those of the pupils under his care rather than those of petulant staff members.

The difficulties with Rothesay Kyle continued unabated, of course, and – sadly – Mr Dick proved of little practical assistance. He had bounced back from the disappointment of his failed interview with a vengeance, and had thrown himself wholeheartedly into a plethora of in-service courses which gave a dedicated promotion-seeker such as himself the chance to escape children on a regular basis, as well as the chance to avoid any staff concerns which might arise. On those rare occasions when he found himself in school, his most recently acquired skill – that of active listening – was to prove of immeasurable benefit. To him.

At least, as Christmas approached, Morris found himself looking forward to the regular bout of staff festivities. It had been decided to forego an outing this year, largely due to the unpleasantness generated during the previous year's Christmas dinner at Rashmani's Restaurant. Instead, a staffroom lunch had been arranged under the direction of Miss Tarbet. Unfortunately, not everyone was pulling their weight.

Monday

Miss Tarbet of home economics has been disappointed at the response to her request for contributions to the staffroom Christmas lunch on Friday. Her attractively designed poster requiring staff to append their names and the dish which they are prepared to make for the occasion has been singularly lacking in suggestions to date, and she made an urgent plea this morning for us all to get into the festive spirit as quickly as possible.

'Huh!' grumbled Mr Pickup, recalling his own role in organising last year's disastrous Christmas dinner. 'As far as I'm concerned, she can whistle! If I remember rightly, Sandra Tarbet did bugger all to help *me* last year, so I don't see why I'm obliged to do anthing for *her*.'

To be honest, I think there was a little bit of sour grapes in Pickup's attitude: ever since he resigned as staff social convenor, he has done nothing but pour scorn on everyone else's attempts to initiate extra-curricular events, and Friday's lunch is simply another in a long line of activities he has chosen to rubbish.

I reprimanded him as politely as I could and added my own name to Morag's list with the offer of three sticks of garlic bread (which I've asked the biology department to cook in their oven) before proffering my £1.50 contribution to cover the cost of liquid refreshments for the day.

'And don't forget to get plenty of red wine,' grumbled Pickup as he eventually agreed to take *some* part in the affair. 'And I hope you've got some water bearers organised for the coffee.'

'Everything's under control, Mr Pickup,' Miss Tarbet replied coolly, as she explained that some first year boys had been delegated to transfer water supplies from the ground floor to the C Floor staffroom in an attempt to ward off the possibility of lead poisoning which might otherwise arise.

To explain, there have been numerous complaints of late concerning the quality of tap-water on offer in the upstairs staffroom, where our Christmas lunch is to be held: serious doubts have been cast upon its purity, given the age of the pipes through which it has to travel to reach our sink, not to mention the storage tanks through which it appears to pass before it reaches our tap, and thereafter our coffee-urn. In short, it tastes revolting, and most staff members now refuse to drink from it, preferring instead to bring in thermos flasks of their own or to transfer supplies from a suitably purified source in the downstairs staffroom. Hence Pickup's request, already anticipated by Sandra Tarbet – much to his chagrin, I suspect.

'Oh,' he muttered. 'Right. Fine. Well, if you don't need any advice, I'll leave you to it, then, Miss Tarbet.'

'Fine, Mr Pickup,' she smiled. 'Just make sure you get your name down for something, that's all – no contribution, no entry, you know!' Pickup just glowered.

Tuesday

More guidance problems with Rothesay O'Brien. Or Kyle, I should say. The poor girl is in the process of changing step-fathers again (for the sixth time in her relatively young life, I am led to believe by her social worker), with the concomitant maternal request that her daughter be henceforth known as Rothesay Kyle.

This is perfectly acceptable to me, and I have issued a guidance circular indicating the mother's wishes. Unfortunately, Mr Dunbar (who has taken an irrational dislike to the girl based upon her tendency to interrupt his maths lessons by banging her head up and down off her desk) has perversely chosen to ignore the request and insists upon calling the register using her previous surname.

'It's no' Roathesay O'Brien, baldy!' she had apparently challenged him yesterday afternoon. 'It's Roathesay Kyle! OK?'

Dunbar's wrath had known no bounds, and he had lost little time in acquainting me with the peremptory rudeness of the girl. I tried to reacquaint him with the concepts of positive and negative reinforcement which I am endeavouring to utilise with Rothesay, but it cut no ice.

'Don't give me all that psychological crap, Simpson!' he cursed. 'Just get the little bitch suspended, OK? And then the rest of the class can get on with some work for a change!'

Dunbar seems completely intolerant over the matter, as I explained to Pickup at afternoon break.

'I'm floundering, Pickup, I don't mind admitting it,' I told him. 'I think I'll have to see Mr Dick again and ask for a ruling on it all.'

'Hah!' he guffawed. 'Take it to him, by all means, Morris, but don't expect a ruling on it before the end of the decade.'

'What d'you mean?' I queried.

'Haven't you noticed? Ever since he went on that active listening course last month, that's all the little fart's been any good at.'

'What?'

'Listening! He'll listen till the proverbial cows come home. But just try and get him to *do* something, to react, to respond – and you might as well forget you're alive, old son. I spent thirty-five minutes last week complaining to him about the number of please-takes I've had this session; and *he* spent the entire time staring sincerely into my eyes, nodding his head and agreeing with every complaint I made – then I come in this morning to find three please-takes for today, all signed by Richard bloody Dick. The man makes me puke, Morris!'

It's hardly a very respectful way to talk about senior staff, and I lost no time in letting Pickup know that I have a good deal more confidence than he has in Mr Dick's abilities to assit me in my guidance remit. After all, that's what he's paid for.

Wednesday

Sought out Mr Dick after morning registration, and acquainted him with my difficulties concerning Rothesay Kyle. Without wishing to support Mr Pickup's contention in any way whatsoever, I found the conversation a little unsettling, to say the least.

'Oh yes?' he nodded solicitously as I told him about Mr Dunbar's unhelpful attitude towards Rothesay.

'Yes,' I confirmed. 'And it's causing severe emotional trauma for Rothesay,' I explained 'Not to mention her mother.'

'Oh really?' he stared deeply into my eyes once more, and I felt forced to turn away.

'And then there's the problem of trying to appear fair to *both* sides,' I sighed uselessly.

'Oh, I know, I know,' he appeared to sympathise. 'Both sides,' he repeated my phrase. 'Of course. Both sides. I see your problem, Morris, I really do ...'

'So you *will* be able to help sort it out?' I eventually put the question.

'Sort it out?' he oozed in further repetition. 'Oh, yes, Morris, I'm sure we'll be able to sort it out eventually – wouldn't you say ...?'

'Um,' I parried, uncertain as to how the initiative had been returned to me instead of him. 'Um – yes, but – um, if you could lend me your support, Richard, then ...'

'Support?' he repeated. 'Always behind you, Morris. Always behind you. As you well know,' he punched me playfully on the shoulder.

'Um ... Thanks, Richard,' I proffered uncertain gratitude. 'Thanks for listening anyway.'

'No problem, Morris,' he smiled unctuously. 'That's what I'm here for, after all ...'

Thursday

Mr Carswell has been ousted as chairman of the school board!

His opting-out ballot last week proved a disastrous failure: he got a 24% turn-out, of which 94% rejected his proposal – a majority which he claimed 'was not necessarily representative of the views of most parents'. This somewhat Jesuitical argument did not wash with other members of the board who had litle hesitation in proposing a vote of no-confidence at last night's meeting with the aforementioned result.

I can't say I'm sorry: the man has caused me – and the school – no little trouble in the past three years, and his arguments about the school being closed if we didn't opt out are beginning to look pretty thin, to be honest: we have the support of several prominent local politicians in our battle to remain open as the educational nerve-centre of Parkland community, and our future looks pretty secure as a result.

Meanwhile, I am more concerned about Mr Dick's failure to deal competently with Mrs O'Brien this afternon. Or rather Mrs Kyle.

The woman apparently came charging up to school prepared to do battle with Mr Dunbar in person over his continued reluctance to accord Rothesay her new-found surname. Mr Dunbar however, was out of school for the day (on a course, of course), so she found herself dealing with Mr Dick instead. Despite my in-depth conversation with the man yesterday afternoon, he apparently denied all knowledge of the case and instead directed the virago of a woman to the precincts of my guidance office.

It would be difficult to convey the depth of feeling which Mrs Kyle had so obviously experienced over the matter, but she left me in little doubt as to what was likely to happen to Mr Dunbar if 'big Tony' (her new common-law husband) ever got to hear of the school's unwillingness to acknowledge the existence of Kyle as an appropriate surname for her daughter. Suffice to say that Mr Dunbar – who has recently taken to singing in a barber-shop quartet during his leisure time – would find himself restricted to the *contralto* section of the group rather than the *basso profundo* for which he has gained such renown.

Friday

The school is to close! Nothing official yet, but a leaked memo to the *Parkland Gazette* would seem to confirm the fact that we are due to merge with Rockston High School as of next August. Obviously, we have had the support of the *wrong* local politicians!

The whole school feels devastated, and the news certainly cast a pall of gloom over today's staff Christmas lunch. Not that it wouldn't have been gloomy enough in the first place, to be honest.

I *had* tried to bring some festive jollity to the occasion by decorating my glasses with some silver tinsel, but the whole affair was disappointingly flat: to begin with, very few members of staff had roused themselves to make any significant contribution to the epicurean delights which were supposed to have been on offer. Apart from my three sticks of garlic bread and Miss Tarbet's egg soufflé, the only other contributions of significant culinary merit were a packet of rich tea biscuits from Mr Pickup, two rice salads from Martin Henderson, a pre-cooked pack of Chinese Chicken from Moira Cunnigham, plus twelve Black Forest Gateaux which had been brought in by twelve different staff, all of them apparently unable to communicate their intentions to each other. And then there was the coffee.

My entire second-year class having failed to turn up for their lesson this morning, I was in the fortunate position of being able to prepare the staffroom for the party. I had just finished stringing some paper chains across the ceiling when two first-year boys arrived at the door.

'This is from Mr Matheson in the downstairs staffroom,' they explained, handing over a large plastic container of water for the post-prandial coffee, in accordance with Miss Tarbert's arrangements. Or so I thought.

'Thanks boys,' I sent them on their way with a cheery Christmas greeting and an exhortation not to be downhearted at the news of their school's imminent closure – not that they seemed bothered, frankly – after which I proceeded to empty the contents of their container into the urn.

It was some two hours later that the consequences of my action became apparent, and it seemed especially ironic that so many of the staff had, by then, recovered a degree of alcohol-induced jollity as a result of Miss Tarbet's bulk-purchasing power at the local cash-and-carry.

'Thatsh shooper value for £1.50,' slurred Mr Pickup, for example, before demanding a 'large black coffee to shober up with', a request which was repeated by several other teachers prior to commencing their last lessons of the term with whatever remnants of their respective classes remained in school by now.

I shall never forget the soporific grin on Pickup's face as he raised the coffee mug to his lips. It was in such stark contrast to the subsequent expression of shock, followed by one of infinite disgust as he sprayed the contents of his mouth across several innocent bystanders.

'BLWAAH!' he scorched angrily. 'What bastard's peed in the coffee?' he bellowed – causing great offence, I might add, to the school chaplain who had kindly joined us after the term's closing service. 'It tastes awful,' Pickup continued, '– what the hell's *in* it?'

It took some time to get to the root of the problem: after initial suspicion had been cast upon the likes of Tommy McShane and Rothesay Kyle, I valiantly pointed out that they could hardly have been responsible as they were illegaly absent from school today – whereupon we got down to the more detailed question of who had been responsible for filling up the urn in the first place ...

It is all a very long story, and for obvious reasons I would rather not go into its most intimate – and abusive – details: suffice to say, had I been made more fully aware that Mr Matheson's message boys had been despatched upon the conveyance of replacment methylated fluid for the staffroom Banda machine, then of course I would never have *dreamt* of inserting it into our coffee-urn. Sadly, they had failed to make themselves clear about the contents of the plastic container which they had given me, and I *still* contend that my assumption of its contents as safe drinking water was a perfectly natural one to make. If sadly mistaken.

It all made for a very dismal end to the term. Pickup still maintains that his subsequent illness in the gents' toilet was solely due to my attempts at mass food-poisoning – a claim of some dubiety, given the amount of wine he had consumed beforehand – while Miss Tarbet took me severely to task as I gave a hand with the dishes afterwards.

'Talk about ruining the Christmas lunch!' she whispered fiercely in my ear as we stood at the sink together. 'For a teacher, Morris, you're a Class One Dickhead! Do you know that? And why don't you take that ridiculous tinsel off your glasses?'

I bit my lip and remained silent. So much for comfort and joy ...

January

There is little to record concerning the Christmas vacation which followed yet another Parkland Christmas party which had failed to live up to expectations – the last, as it was to befall. As on many a Christmas holiday before, Morris Simpson found himself looking back – with regret – to the previous term, and looking forward – with trepidation – to the term about to commence.

Although Mr Ross tried to keep everyone's end up, so to speak, Morris was not alone in his depression.

Monday

An air of despondency hangs over the school following the region's final (final) decision to close us down next June.

'It's not a closure,' the headmaster tried to convince us at a staff meeting in the lecture theatre this afternoon. 'It's a *merger* of Parkland High with Rockston High, and we should all see it as a tremendous new challenge, a chance to start afresh in a dynamic educational adventure.'

He isn't fooling anyone, least of all the parents, many of whom have now transferred their offspring to Freeman Secondary, a more prestigious establishment outwith our catchment area altogether, with the result that our roll is now at its lowest ever level of 231 (including the school cat), indicating profound parental discontent at the prospect of their children attending our yet-to-be-named, newly-merged school.

'Hah,' whispered Mr Pickup, sitting beside me in the back row. 'Dynamic educational adventure my backside! Never mind not having enough pupils to fill both of the old schools, the way things are going I doubt if we'll have enough to fill a combined *new* one! It's all very well the rats leaving the sinking ship, but this time they're doing it before the bloody thing's been launched!'

Other symptoms of our educational decline include the disbandment of the school board: in their enthusiasm to oust the chairman before Christmas, the other board members neglected to realise that his departure left them without sufficient parental membership to satisfy the terms of their constitution. Having been unable to find a replacement, they have instead decided to throw in the towel. I can't say I blame them.

Tuesday

Despite our imminent closure – or merger, rather – we are expected to carry on teaching as if nothing extraordinary has happened, or was going to happen. My pedagogical life continues to be made well-nigh impossible because of the appalling and continuing leaks in the roof of Hut A57 – at least I can leave *that* behind when we move to Rockston – as well as the guidance dilemma occasioned by Rothesay O'Brien's change of surname. Mr Dunbar of maths is proving intractable in his declared intention of refusing to call the girl Rothesay Kyle – 'if *she* won't co-operate with *me*, then I don't see why *I* should co-operate with *her*' – despite last month's warning of retribution from the mother's new common-law husband (a man who apparently goes by the name of 'Big Tony'). It was his somewhat bulky arrival upon the matrimonial scene which has led to the request for a change of Rothesay's surname upon the school register.

The warning was repeated to me by the girl herself when she arrived at my guidance office during morning interval.

'Surr!' she beseeched me. 'Goanny tell Mistur Dunbar that if he dusny stoap callin' me Roathesay O'Brien, then big Tony sez he's goanny get a right doin'!' She was most distraught, but I managed to calm her down by assuring her that I would speak to Mr Dunbar about the matter, after which I earnestly suggested that she attempt to restrain her new stepfather's more intimidatory instincts.

Unfortunately, our pastoral conversation was cut short because I had to meet up with Mr & Mrs Knox, who were in attendance to complain most volubly about the stop-gap timetabling measures which the school has had to adopt since the departure of Mr Ferguson, our erstwhile job-sharing principal teacher of modern languages.

Sadly, they were indisposed to listen to my explanation of why their daughter has only had a French teacher every alternate week for the last two months, preferring instead to demand immediate action. On that count, at least, I was able to pass on good news, having just been told by Mr Dick that a supply teacher had at last been arranged to cover for Mr Ferguson's timetable.

'A what?' enquired Mr Knox suspiciously.

'A supply teacher,' I explained patiently, 'has been arranged to take over Mr Ferguson's half of the teaching timetable. I'm sorry about the long delay, but the headmaster's had difficulty in getting a replacement teacher to join us.'

'Oh,' he said, temporarily mollified, before muttering under his breath, 'I'm not surprised. Who'd want to teach *here*?'

I pretended not to hear this unconscionably rude remark, and brought the interview to a conclusion by assuring them that their daughter would henceforth be treated to a full and varied diet of absorbing and instructive French lessons from now until the end of the session.

'Well, that'll be a change,' he fired a parting shot. 'She certainly never got *that* when Ferguson was here.'

I ignored the comment once more and asked him to close the door behind him.

Wednesday

Today saw the departure – on maternity leave – of Fiona Pratt. It was with mixed emotions that I wished her well for the last few weeks of her pregnancy: once the object of my own affections, the pang of slight desire which I still experience for her was nevertheless tinged with bitterness at the unwholesome lack of taste she has displayed in her choice of soul-mate: Martin Pratt, the unbelievably recalcitrant pony-tailed history student who was with us last year.

Nobly, I bit back by emotions, wished her 'all the best, and,' – I smiled as convincingly as I could – 'to Martin as well,' before attempting a brief embrace, an ill-considered venture considering her ample girth, and one which saw me bending awkwardly forward across her 'bump' for a swift peck on the cheek.

'OK, Morris,' she looked away with evident distaste and waddled slowly out of the staffroom.

I sighed profoundly with thoughts of what might have been, and turned instead to ask Mr Dick for some further advice on the touchy quetion of Rothesay Kyle and her belligerent step-father.

Infuriatingly, our assistant head is still intent upon practising his active listening skills and I realised once again that not a single word of what I was saying had been taken in.

'Oh really, Morris,?' he oozed charm and concern. It's just too bad, isn't it?'

'Well, yes,' I explained patiently. 'It's an impossible situation for me, being caught between the family and Mr Dunbar, and –'

'Oh, I know, Morris,' he assured me. 'I hear what you're saying. And I know what you mean, I really do …' he tailed off.

I stared in uncomprehending frustration. 'Ohh – ff … ff – forget it!' I burst out, and started to make my way towards the staffroom door when who should walk in but Martin Pratt! I jumped guiltily.

'Oh! Um – hello, Martin,' I tried to raise a welcoming smile. 'What are *you* doing here? In to pick up Fiona, eh?'

He raised his eyes heavenward with the natural insolence for which I remembered him so well. 'Nope,' he tossed back at me. 'In to pick up my timetable –'

'Your what?' I queried him, puzzled.

'My timetable,' he repeated patiently. 'You know. For teaching. I'm starting here tomorrow – supply-teacher in place of Mr Ferguson.'

'You're what? But you can't. He was a French teacher. And you're a –' I paused and looked him up and down, wondering how carefully I should choose my words. 'And you're a history teacher,' I concluded lamely.

'Well done, Mr Simpson,' he clapped in elaborate sarcasm. 'Ten out of ten. Now has anyone seen old Toddy?' he wandered out of the door in disrespectful search of our depute head.

'But that's ridiculous!' I exploded to Mr Dick, who was still standing nearby. 'We need a French teacher and he's a history teacher. What am I going to tell Mr Knox? It's ridiculous!' I appealed again.

Mr Dick looked pensive, and I thought for one minute he was going to make an original remark. 'Mmm,' he nodded. 'You're right, Morris. Exactly right. And I hear what you're saying. It's a problem, isn't it? Let's talk about it sometime. Eh?'

I sighed once more, shut my eyes, and sat down. Under the circumstances, it just seemed the best thing to do.

Thursday

Unbelievably, some workmen have arrived to repair my roof! The last such renovative expenditure by the education authority was just under four years ago, and in the past three and a half of these years the glorified Nissen hut which I share with Mr Pickup has been subject to endless instances of further leakage, all of them repeatedly reported to the works department, and all of them repeatedly ignored.

It seems ironic that they've finally got round to doing something about it, only six months before the place is to close, and I was saying as much to Mr Pickup as we viewed the workmen ascending our roof after morning break.

'Ah, that's nothing, Simpson,' chortled Mr Pickup. 'The best ever was when they sent the painters in to do a complete renovation job on St Anthony's. Remember?'

I had to plead ignorance, so Pickup continued: 'Ahh – that was a classic. Paint peeling off the walls, paint peeling off the window frames and paint peeling off the woodwork – what was left of it, at any rate. Never been touched by brush nor roller in half a century – until they announced it was to close. Four days later, the council sends in a hit-squad of forty painters on their rolling maintenance programme – it rolled every 25 years, if I remember rightly – and the national papers were down there after them like a shot. He drew an imaginary headline across the air: "Doomed School Is Painted: Gross Waste of Public Money!" or some such nonsense, complete with photographs to match. Ah,' he sighed reflectively. 'A real classic. If only ...' he pondered quietly. 'Ach!' he suddenly snapped himself back to reality. 'Too much to hope for, I suppose – but this is still pretty good value, don't you think?' he pointed to the workmen on the roof. 'What say I give the Parkland Gazette a ring?'

I told him not to be so unprofessional and hurried off to my guidance office to catch up on some pastoral review work. In retrospect, I wished I hadn't, because waiting at my desk – in *my* seat, mark you – was an awesomely framed figure of fearsome appearance and glowering countenance. Mr Kyle, I realised at once: it was just as well that Mr Dunbar was away on a course again, I reflected, as I gauged the enormous physical dimensions before me.

'Good morning, Mr – er?' I hedged for time.

'Kyle!' he jumped to his feet and barked from behind an angrily twitching moustache, before launching into an impassioned and furious explanation for his visit. Unfortunately, the precise meaning of his words was veiled by an accent which was so completely impenetrable that I found it difficult to follow his drift. Apart from the frequent use of phrases such as 'sleekit wee Dickie bastudd' (which I took to be a reference to our assistant head) and 'effin' big chubeface' (which I immediately recognised as Mr Dunbar) I was completely at a loss. Eventually, I decided to follow Mr Dick's tactic of active listening, and was gratified by its immediate success.

'Oh yes?' I mutttered at discreet intervals, or 'Oh no?' when the

tone of his voice seemed to warrant it. And 'Oh really?' as often as I could. It all appeared to have a fairly calming effect on the man, who eventually ran out of vituperative steam and left the room with my assurance ringing in his ears that I would 'deal with it at the earliest opportunity.'

Perhaps I should see Mr Dick for a few more tips: there's obviously more to this 'active listening' than meets the eye. Or ear.

Friday

Arrived at the school gates this morning to find Pickup in a high state of agitation.

'Quickly, Morris! Come quickly!' he urged me across the playground and around the back of the school. 'We've hit the jackpot!'

Uncertain of his meaning, I followed him around the school to witness several sets of white overcoats in the process of erecting scaffolding. A quick glance at the van from which they were removing the metal tubing revealed that they were from the Parkland Weathershield and Maintenance Company, while a quick glance at Pickup's excited features revealed that one of his wildest fantasies had actually been fulfilled.

'Bingo!' he raised both fists in the air. 'Brilliant, isn't it? They've sent the painters in after all! I *knew* we could depend on them! I've sent for the *Parkland Gazette*, of course, but in the meantime ...' Pickup withdrew a camera from his jacket pocket and started to snap at will, even asking for an occasional pose from myself and the first year boys who by now had started a series of armed conflicts using the scaffolding's metal connecting bolts as weapons.

'I'm compiling a scrapbook of the school's history,' he announced cheerily as he asked a painter to hold still for a moment, 'and this is for the final section.'

'Oh, that'll be nice,' I commented, uncertain whether Pickup was fully in control of himself or not. 'What'll it be called, your scrapbook?'

He thought briefly, then announced with sweeping grandeur: 'Parkland High School: the Glory Years!'

I just hope he can find enough material.

February

Sadly, Mr Pickup's hopes of a publicity fanfare surrounding the redecoration of the doomed Parkland High were not to be realised, as was revealed in Simpson's next diary entry. The lack of media coverage was a source of keen disappointment to Pickup, but his regrets were as nothing compared to the dismay experienced by Morris upon learning the identity of Mr Ferguson's supply-replacement.

As we have already learned, Morris had developed a certain antipathy towards Martin Pratt: it was based largely upon their earlier meetings during Pratt's student days, and had been further exacerbated by Pratt's subsequent marriage to Fiona Strangelove. However, Simpson's main and continuing source of grievance towards Pratt was more concerned with the man's attitude towards his work, and towards supply-teaching in particular.

And things weren't made any easier by the increasing intractability of Mr and Mrs Knox. The diary extract for February explains the matter in greater detail.

Monday

Who'd be a guidance teacher? An awkward telephone call from Mrs Knox this morning concerning the non-provision of appropriate French lessons for her daughter. Despite my recent assurances that Samantha would soon be receiving full tuition in the subject, I have been cast adrift by the staffing department's decision to send a newly-qualified history teacher on supply instead of the linguistically competent replacement which I had expected for Mr Ferguson.

'Mrs Knox?' I said to Sandra, our switchboard operator, when told who was on the other end of the line. 'Oh, for heaven's sake, tell her I can't be reached – I haven't got the time to listen to any more of her ruddy complaints about the French department –'

'Pardon?' snapped the distinctly angry voice of Mrs Knox from the earpiece. Unfortunately, Sandra had already put the call through, and I had a slightly embarrassing few moments before I hit on the idea of telling Mrs Knox that I thought the call had been from the modern languages adviser instead of her good self.

'Huh!' she barked down the line. 'So the modern languages adviser's got complaints about the French department as well, has she? Well, I'm not surprised!' she declaimed, as she launched into yet another tirade of abuse directed at the fact that Samantha's class has been lacking any kind of effective education in modern languages during the weeks when Mrs Leleu – the other half of the job-share – is not in school. In particular, she wished to make her views plain on the appalling attitude displayed by Martin Pratt, our pony-tailed history supply teacher, whom she described as 'a highly-paid babysitter!'

She claimed, among other things, that he spent every lesson with Samantha's French class simply sitting at the front of the room reading his newspaper and advsing them they could 'do as they wished as long as they didn't make too much noise'.

This all seemed rather exaggerated to my ears: I mean, I know I'm not terribly fond of young Mr Pratt, but even *he* wouldn't be as unprofessional as that! I have promised to investigate and report back.

Tuesday

Mr Pickup continues to gather material for his commemorative scrapbook compilation to mark the forthcoming closure of our school. Provisionally entitled 'Parkland High – The Glory Years', the publication looks set to be a fairly cynical volume comprising a sardonic glimpse down the ages of academic misdemeanour for which the school has been so amply renowned in years past.

By way of illustration, he gave me a preview this morning of his magazine's section devoted to 'News of Former Pupils': this tribute to our former alumni was composed almost entirely of newspaper clippings from the police and court report pages of the *Parkland Gazette*. Therein were to be found the embarrassingly frequent court appearances of several local worthies, all former charges of Parkland High, and all now apparently intent upon pursuing a life of sordid debauchery and crime.

Gary Sinnott, for example – of whose school career I still have most painful recollection – seems to have made no fewer than fourteen court appearances in the two and a half years since he left our educational ministrations. The charges have ranged from the fairly standard drunk-and-disorderly (four separate occasions and a total of fifteen months' community service arising therefrom) to the somewhat bizarre details surrounding Sinnott's misguided and libidinous attempts to set up a massage parlour in the unlikely environs of Parkland Crescent, utilising the services of selected former classmates as employees.

Sadly missing from Pickup's newspaper file was any front-page splash of the school being repainted some five months prior to closure: the newspaper coverage had to be abandoned owing to the hasty departure from the scene of the Parkland Weathershield and Maintenance Company some fifty minutes after their arrival last month. Alas, a staffroom mole (rumoured to be Richard Dick, our assistant head) had been on the telephone to the regional offices upon discovering the works department's error, with the result that no less a person than the Director of Education himself had telephoned back in double-quick time – with a frankly-worded injunction that they 'get that bloody paint-van out of the playground before the papers get hold of this one'.

Despite Pickup's disloyal attempts to have the *Parkland Gazette* round in time, the photographer arrived just as the last of the scaffolding had been dismantled and the pictureless story was relegated to an inside column of the newspaper. Needless to say, Pickup's attempts to sell his own Polaroid records of the occasion were rejected on the grounds of the excessive payment demanded by my colleague for the snaps in question – not to mention some very shaky focusing.

Wednesday

Shocked to dicover that Mrs Knox has strong grounds for complaint!

I sneaked a look through the classroom window of B15 this morning to witness a scene almost entirely reminiscent of the one described in her telephone call on Monday. There was Pratt, feet up on his desk, scanning a newspaper, while every member of the class was engaged in what I could only describe as free verbal activity – and not a jotter in sight!

Even when I went into the classroom on the pretext of asking for some guidance details, he made no attempt to look industrious, and simply answered my query about the class's work-rate with the response that it was 'nothing to do with him'.

I took him severely to task at morning interval, and reminded him of how he should be spending his time with each class under his care.

'What d'you mean?' he looked at me, astonished. 'What d'you mean, teach them?'

'Teach them!' I repeated my words of advice. 'That's what you're being paid to do, not sitting around reading a newspaper like a ... a –' I searched for the right expression, but couldn't better Mrs Knox's description of his babysitting activities.

'But that's exactly what I am!' he admitted in shameless aggression. 'A highly paid child-minder! Trained for five years, only to walk into a complete black hole of employment: I've been on supply-teaching since the day I started, Simpson, and the way things are going, I'll be on supply-teaching till the day I stop! And I wouldn't particularly mind if I was supplying in my own subject, but d'you know how many history lessons I've taught since last August?'

'Um – thirty, forty?' I wondered.

'Four,' he explained angrily. 'And two of *them* were to a geography class that got sent into the wrong room by mistake! So don't give me your precious words of advice about preparing aims and objectives and lesson plans for every bloody rag-bag of a class I'm unfortunate enough to get lumbered with. As far as I'm concerned, I don't give a toss what they do as long as they don't make too much noise!'

'But where's your sense of vocation, your sense of *reward* in that type of approach?' I made a final effort to persuade him.

'Reward?' he smirked a supercilious grin as he fingered his ridiculous ear-ring. 'Haven't you heard about the daily payment rates for babysitting – er – supply-teaching, Mr Simpson?' he corrected himself. 'Roughly double your own rate of reward, I think ...'

I shook my head in disbelief at such a mercenary attitude and mentally gave thanks that his job-sharing partner was due in this afternoon. Unfortunately, Mr Tod chose this moment to arrive in the staffroom and announce the fact that Mrs Leleu has been struck down with the debilitating virus which has already affected nearly half the staff this month, and which will ensure her absence for at least the next seven days.

'We're completely stuck, Martin,' he pleaded with Pratt. 'You couldn't help us out, could you?'

I could almost see Pratt's greedy little cash-register eyes ringing up the totals in advance as he agreed to another week of over-paid indolence.

'Of course, Mr Tod,' he concurred with ill-concealed pleasure. 'As long as I can change my afternoon shift in the pub for the next few days, there shouldn't be any problem.'

I couldn't believe it! To think of the money the taxpayer's spent on training the man, and he ends up reading newspapers in a classroom for one week, then serving in a pub the next! It's a disgrace – and for the life of me, I can't think how I'll explain the situation to Mrs Knox.

Thursday

More guidance troubles. At 10 am this morning, Alan McLeary was marked absent from his social education class, only to be found later on behind the bicycle sheds with a can of hairspray and assorted polythene bags, the intended purposes for which I am frightened to hazard a guess.

Meanwhile, there is the continuing dilemma over Rothesay Kyle, whose new step-father has been making unpleasantly intimidating threats to Mr Dunbar of maths. Rothesay has grown even more disturbed as a result, and has started to throw uncontrollable fits of temper in practically every class she attends.

As their guidance teacher I am, of course, held personally responsible for such misbehaviour, so it was with understandable enthusiasm that I jumped at our educational psychologist's offer this afternoon of two places at a residential holiday-farm for any of my pastoral charges whom I considered likely to benefit from such an experience.

'Rothesay Kyle and Alan McLeary!' I shouted in excited relief. 'Just to get rid of them for – uh – yes,' I took control of myself and decided it wiser to expound my enthusiasm for the scheme in a more relaxed and professional manner. 'Um – sorry,' I continued. 'What I meant to say was that – um – I think both children would benefit from that kind of, uh, short-term exposure to an altered environmental structure.'

'My words exactly,' smiled Mr Boyd. 'I'll set it up for next month, then?'

'Yes,' I nodded enthusiastically. 'Oh yes. Yes please ...'

Friday

A very satisfying end to the week.

To explain, Martin Henderson of history failed to arrive in school this morning, having succumbed to the same mystery virus as Mrs Leleu and practically half the rest of the staff. His absence meant that our staffing levels were dangerously inadequate, and for once the staffing department responded with a degree of urgency to Mr Tod's request that they send a body – any body – around to bring our complement up to a manageable level.

Interestingly enough, I couldn't help but notice that Mrs Johnston's approach to her temporary task was in sharp contrast to Martin Pratt's – just before morning interval I had to see one of her third-year pupils about an incident of theft, and was amazed to discover her hard at work on a medieval history project which Martin had started with the class on Tuesday.

'That's a nice change,' I spoke to her at morning break. 'At least they've sent a history teacher for a history supply – must be some mistake!' I laughed at my own litle joke.

'Oh they haven't,' she explained seriously. 'And I'm not.'

'Sorry?'

'I'm not a history teacher. But the stuff was all there, and it seemed fairly straightforward, so I just got on with it. Otherwise you'd get bored, wouldn't you, just sitting reading newspapers or something?'

I glanced sharply across at Martin Pratt in the hope that he'd been listening. Unfortunately, he was asleep.

'That's fascinating,' I returned to Mrs Johnston. 'So what *do* you teach?'

‘French,’ she smiled back at me. ‘But I haven’t had a French class for – ooh –’ she mused ‘– must be at least fourteen months now. Still,’ she concluded, ‘Mustn’t grumble. At least the pay’s good.’

‘Yes,’ I concurred bitterly, before pondering her revelation more deeply. ‘Look,’ I queried sharply, ‘– what did you say you taught?’

‘French,’ she looked surprised at my sharpness. ‘Why?’

‘Oh, nothing,’ I called back as I scurried off in search of Mr Dick to suggest a swift rearrangement of our respective supply teachers’ responsibilities – and timetables.

Unfortunately, our assistant head’s active listening skills remain irredeemably inert (‘Mmm. Good idea,’ he congratulated me, before wandering off in complete ignorance of what I’d just said), so I took the suggestion to Mr Tod, our depute head.

‘So let me get this right, Simpson,’ he quizzed me. You say Mrs Johnston’s a French teacher who’s been sent to cover a history supply; while Pratt’s a history teacher who’s covering a French supply?’

‘That’s right,’ I confirmed. ‘So why can’t we –’

‘Of course!’ he clenched both fists in realisation. ‘That’s a tremendous idea, Simpson. Especially for someone with your record of moronic initiatives!’ My irritation at this unnecessary additional remark was alleviated by his metaphorical suggestion to ‘take fourteen brownie points – you deserve them! At least it’ll keep that bloody Knox woman happy: she’s been buggering me about all morning with precious Samantha and her ruddy French lessons!’

‘But that’s what it’s all about, Mr Tod,’ I reminded him enthusiastically. ‘Satisfying the customer to the best of our abilities – and educating the pupils with the best means at our disposal.’

He looked sceptically over his glasses at me.

‘Aye, Simpson,’ he laughed scornfully. ‘That *will* be right …’

March

It is not unusual, these days, for teachers and educationists to speak of pupils and parents in terms of their being 'customers' rather than simply pupils and parents. The growing emergence of 'management-speak' illustrates the increasing influence of industrial standards and applications in educational provision: quality assurance, time management and performance indicators are fast becoming as common in the classroom as they are in the boardroom, and it is with such factors in mind that many newspapers have revived the practice of publishing examination league tables along with the – ostensible – claim that they are doing so to make parents fully aware of which schools provide the 'best service'. In truth, however, it is likely that the motives of the *Parkland Gazette* in publishing such a table were less concerned with the ethos of public service than with an attempt to boost flagging sales: there is nothing like a schools league table to get readers buying papers again.

It has to be recorded, once again, that those pupils under the tutelage of of Morris Simpson had not improved the average pass-rate of Parkland Community High; quite the reverse, in fact. However, Morris continued to defend his – and the school's – academic endeavours by highlighting the extremely deprived backgrounds experienced by such a large percentage of their charges.

And few were as deprived as Rothesay Kyle and Alan McLeary. Their departure for the Hollydown residential experience had certainly lightened Morris's guidance workload for the month of March, although he still experienced antagonism from the more intractable members of staff – such as Mr Dunbar or Mr Pickup – who persistently failed to appreciate the potential benefits offered by a holistic and pastoral approach to behaviour modification.

In this, as in so many other aspects of school life, Morris sometimes felt he was fighting a losing battle. His diary for March takes up the story.

Monday

Depression abounds. School morale, already at an all-time low due to our impending closure, has been dealt a further body blow by the *Parkland Gazette*'s double-page feature on the recently released examination league tables.

Unsurprisingly, Parkland Community High failed to feature in the upper quartiles of this damning document; indeed, we even failed to merit a statistical mention owing to the fact that under 5% of our senior-school population concluded their education here with three or more Higher grade examination passes. Our only consolation – and a dubious one at that – was the fact that Rockston High (with whom we are due to merge this August) had conspired to achieve the lowliest placing of all, two beneath our own, on this mischievous and misleading measure of educational attainment.

And to make matters worse, Mr Pickup has compiled a league table of his *own*, copies of which he had seen fit to distribute among staff pigeon-holes first thing this morning. Briefly, it indicates his continuing interest in the post-compulsory-schooling experiences of our former pupils as culled from the court reports which regularly appear in the *Parkland Gazette*; Pickup's highly individualistic league table therefore comprises a percentage listing of those schools in the area known to have provided the local and national detainment centres with the bulk of their population over the past four years. Any conviction resulting in a custodial prison sentence of three or more months has been consequently entered into his scoring system, and – after careful checking of the miscreant's *alma mater* – my overly cynical coleague has seen fit to compile the aforementioned document which, he claims, should at last provide some long-awaited solace to our hard-pressed senior management team.

I just had to challenge him on that one, but he opened his eyes wide in innocence.

'Of course it should cheer them up!' he protested enthusiastically. 'It's the first league table we've been top of for thirty years!'

Tuesday

The headmaster does not appear to share Pickup's twisted sense of humour, and has ordered the immediate destruction of all documents bearing his infamous league tables.

'Ach,' muttered Pickup, screwing up the sternly-worded rectorial memo which he had just received. 'The old fart just can't see a joke.'

'Well, I have to say I agree with him on this one, Mr Pickup,' I chastised him. 'I mean it's the easiest thing in the world to take raw data like this and portray all these statistics as the school's fault – but just *look* at the social deprivation these kids have to put up with! Over half of our children are from single parent families, and –'

'Oh, for God's sake, Simpson!' he exploded. 'And so were half the war-children from *my* generation from single-parent families, but that didn't mean they went round robbing pensioners and setting schools on fire for their leisure-time activities! And another thing –' he seemed about to launch into another tirade before checking himself, sighing, and shaking a weary head.

'Ah, forget it, Morris,' he sighed. 'I just don't think I can be bothered any more, that's all. The fun's all gone out of it these days.'

It was the most serious I'd ever seen him; for a moment, I was worried at the awkward pause which prevailed, but he soon came round again, and the outburst seemed forgotten.

'Anyway,' he smiled wanly, '– talking of social deprivation, how are Rothesay Kyle and Alan McLeary getting on?'

'Great!' I enthused. 'The fortnight at Hollydown Holiday Farm seems to be doing them the world of good, from all I can hear. Their educational psychologist was out there yesterday and says he's seen a dramatic improvement in their interpersonal dynamics, not to mention the social cohesion they're beginning to experience.'

Pickup snorted briefly before warning me that not all members of staff shared my enthusiasm for the psychological benefits likely to be experienced by the two worst-behaved pupils in my guidance section.

'And I can't say I blame them, Simpson,' he confided quietly across the coffee table. 'I mean, it's all very well getting the little bastards out of *our* hair for a fortnight, but Mark Dunbar, for one, reckons it's a bit thick if the only reward Rothesay Kyle gets for all the abuse she's heaped on him this year is to go off for a fortnight's free donkey rides!'

'Oh, for heaven's sake!' I defended my guidance initiative stoutly. 'That just goes to show how little any of you understand about pastoral relationships, Pickup.' He snorted again, but I wouldn't be deflected. 'The whole point of allocating these short-term educational holidays to problem children is to give them *trust*, to give them *opportunity*, to give them a glimpse of what education can *do* for them if they give it a chance. And for pupils like Alan McLeary, it means the chances of full integration into a mainstream timetable are improved beyond belief.'

'Integration for Alan McLeary?' Pickup questioned, looking over his glasses with stern reprimand, even warning, in his voice. 'It's not *inte*gration that McLeary needs, in my opinion.'

'Oh? What is it then?' I foolishly walked into his trap.

'It's *cas*tration, Simpson. That's what someone like Alan McLeary needs. Vicious litle toad that he is,' he muttered, before sitting back to finish his coffee, a wicked smile of imaginative cruelty creeping slowly across his face.

At least, that way, I knew he was back to his old self again ...

Wednesday

Supply-teaching morale has improved a great deal since my innovative suggestion last month that Mr Tod rearrange timetables to ensure that the history and modern languages replacement teachers actually got to teach their own subjects. Mrs Johnston, in particular, having spent the last 14 months teaching anything but French, has relished the chance to get to grips with some linguistic exploration for a change.

Not so happy, of course, is Martin Pratt, our pony-tailed history supply: clearly, the unusual demands being made of him in having to implement lesson plans instead of sit around reading newspapers at the front of the class have left him somewhat drained, hence – I suspect – his absence from school this morning with what he imaginatively termed 'a virus' when reporting the illness by telephone.

Of even greater novelty, therefore, was the sudden call to the breach of the headmaster to teach a lesson with one of Pratt's fourth year classes this morning. Martin Henderson, our (acting) principal teacher of history, recalled our depute's importation of the news with wry amusement at lunchtime:

'Big shock waves at 9.30 am all right! Tod's on the internal 'phone telling me that his lordship's actually condescended to have a please-take dished out to him on the grounds of no other available personnel – "and make sure you've got plenty of work for them," he tells me. "No group activities or discussions, mark you: he wouldn't know where to start. Just give them plenty of worksheets – or better still, some books and jotters – and enough questions to do them till Christmas"!'

Clearly, the history department was in no position to embark upon the sudden bulk issue of jotters – rumour has it that none have been seen in the department since the first phase of Standard grade implementation – but this omission apart, Mr Ross's cover lesson appears to have passed off without incident. Apart, that is, from a slightly awkward moment at the beginning:

'Hullo?' a class member had apparently questioned the arrival of his headmaster at the door. 'Who are you?'

Fortunately, Mr Ross had thought it a little joke and laughed the whole matter off. As suspected by Martin Henderson – and as subsequent interrogation of the youth revealed – Peter Watson's enquiry had been all too seriously inclined.

'Well, how wis ah tae know?' Watson had pleaded to Henderson, not unreasonably. 'First time ah've seen the auld shitebag since first yeer wisn't it? An' he's pit oan the beef since then!'

Helpless with mirth, Henderson had issued a punishment

exercise forthwith – and escaped into the storecupboard to give unfettered vent to his hilarity.

Thursday

There is a good deal of concern about the eventual allocation of jobs in our newly-merged school next August. Who will remain? And – more importantly – who is to go? For myself, I have every confidence of remaining in my relatively humble post of (acting) APT guidance, but there is a good deal of jockeying for position amongst the higher echelons, in evidence of which Mr Dick was absent today on yet another course – on team-building, I believe – whilst Monica Cunningham has made clear her own intentions of attaining the single promoted computing post at our new school by signing up for an assertiveness course over the next six weeks.

'God almighty,' Mr Pickup shook his head when he heard the news. 'Monica Cunningham on an assertiveness course?' he queried. 'That's a bit like teaching a rottweiller to bite, isn't it? God save me from pushy women!'

I don't think Pickup's heard of the Equal Opportunities Commission. And I sincerely hope *they* don't get to hear of *him*.

Friday

Mr Boyd, the school's educational psychologist, arrived in the staffroom at morning break, the bearer of mixed tidings.

Initially, of course, I was delighted to hear of the enthusiasm with which Rothesay Kyle and Alan McLeary had entered into their educational rehabilitation at Hollydown Holiday Farm. More unsettling, however, was the news that Rothesay had become so irredeemably attached to a family of rabbits there that she had seen fit to request their permanent removal to the Kyle household upon her planned departure for home this morning.

The request was denied, despite her earnest pleadings to the contrary ('Ah've goat a hutch, but!' she had informed the project co-ordinator, Sonia McEwan), and as a consequence she had taken it upon herself to abscond with all twelve rabbits last night, thereby initiating a staff alert of dramatic proportions. McLeary, of course, had gone with her, though not before the pair of them had deceitfully presented the farm staff with a 'last-night-thank-you-gift' consisting of their own, home-baked, self-labelled 'Choklut Krispies' – liberally dosed, alas, with a laxative of alarming strength and effectiveness.

The staff, understandably disturbed upon discovering the pair's premature departure later on that evening, were nevertheless unable to give full attention to the organisation of a search-party owing to the severe gastric and lavatorial disorders which they were experiencing at the time.

'And things didn't get any easier when McLeary returned after midnight,' continued Mr Boyd sorrowfully, 'with the sole purpose of launching an arson attack on the hen-run. If Sonia McEwan hadn't been up at the toilet at the time, goodness knows what would have happened. Fortunately, only half of the hen-house was destroyed, and there were no serious injuries except for a few singed feathers.'

'But that's appalling!' I exclaimed. 'What on earth –'

'Well, it is and it isn't,' replied Boyd in measured tones. 'Actually, it's all a fairly interesting example of a kind of reverse affection syndrome.'

'Sorry?'

'Reverse affection. "You-always-hurt-the-one-you-love" kind of thing. I mean, the holiday was a great *success* in many terms –

for example the social bonding and the peer-group interaction which Kyle and McLeary have experienced could well make a tremendous attitudinal difference in their future behaviour.'

I tried to interrupt, but Boyd continued regardless.

'You see, the previous lack of affection in Rothesay's life has suddenly been replaced by a concrete expression of an emotion which she's tried to articulate by the only means at her disposal. McLeary, for his part, seems to have found someone at last with whom he can *share* an enthusiasm. Now, for a boy who's previously only displayed *negative* attributes during any raw-score assessments on our personality inventories, I think that's something to be celebrated, and I've said as much to the farm staff this morning.'

'You've seen them about this, then?' I asked needlessly.

'Oh yes,' Mr Boyd nodded his head enthusiastically. 'And Sonia McEwan and Derek Jones are in full agreement. After they'd cleared up the mess we had a complete case review, and we're very confident about the future prospects for Rothesay and Alan being able to internalise their responses to the kind of reactional interface which, previous to the holiday, would have culminated in further disorientation.'

'Reactional *what*?' I enquired in bewilderment.

'Interfaces,' he repeated.

I must have looked bemused, because Boyd clenched his fists in happy proclamation: 'Stop worrying, Mr Simpson: Rothesay and Alan are on an upward learning curve, and it was *your* decision to send them on this holiday that's put them there!'

'And what about the rabbit theft, the chocolate laxatives and the arson attack?' I queried, incredulous at the man's sophistry.

'Serious lapses, yes,' he admitted, 'but we have to look at these incidents in the wider context of the rehabilitation experience, Mr Simpson. I mean, the reason Rothesay and Alan *did* these things was largely because they *loved* the farm so much! In a sense, the theft and the arson attack were attempts to maintain the holiday-farm experience as their own, not to be shared by anybody else in the future – and if we've even got Rothesay and Alan to express some kind of affection, some kind of appreciation – no matter how misguided that expression proved to be – then I think it really means we're *getting* somewhere in our attempts to integrate them fully into mainstream schooling.'

I was speechless at Boyd's suggestion that such liberating and (literally) inflammatory activities could be interpreted as a successful indication of rehabilitaion. Not so Mr Pickup, who had guffawed his way through most of Boyd's previous monologue.

'Hah!' he exploded. 'So you really think Alan McLeary's a candidate for integration do you, Mr Boyd?'

'I do indeed, Mr Pickup,' nodded Boyd, unaware of the alternative forms of behaviour modification expressed to me by Pickup on Tuesday.

'What did I tell you, Morris? Give them trust? Give them opportunity?' Pickup threw my own words back in my face, after which he began an elaborate mime which involved making a spherical cupping motion with his left hand, and drawing an imaginary knife from his breast pocket with the other. Suddenly, swiftly, he made a threefold series of chopping motions which left me in no doubt about the actions which *he* would prefer to take in rehabilitating Alan McLeary.

Understandably, Mr Boyd looked puzzled. For my own part, I began to wonder if Pickup's got a point. No pun intended.

April

PARKLAND HIGH CLOSURE STAKES:

TEACHERS FOR THE CHOP

Mr Major	2/1 on
Mrs Tarbet	10/1
Mr Ross	5/1
Mr Pratt (Supply)	3/1
Mr Crumley	7/1

Simpy

Despite his disappointment over the arson attack at Hollydown Holiday farm, Morris remained firmly committed to the concept of taking an active role in improving the behaviour of pupils such as Alan McLeary. In fact, especially Alan McLeary. Frankly, he couldn't believe Pickup's suggestion that McLeary was simply a 'personification of evil' and that as such he merely represented the latest in a long line of similarly demonic pupils to come before his presence at Parkland High.

Rather, Morris considered that – instead of appealing to McLeary himself – he would be better advised to speak directly with the parents to try to get to the root of the problem, and it was with such thoughts in mind that he accepted a request – received, it must be said, with some surprise – from Mr and Mrs McLeary for a meeting. At last, he reckoned, here would be a chance to discuss their son's attitudinal approaches in a frank and earnest manner.

Mr Pickup, as will be discovered, was aghast at the arrangement, but discovered it too late for alteration to be made. In any case, he had concerns of his own: since the school's impending closure had been announced, morale had plummetted lower with every passing week, and most staff members had grown weary of discussion concerning the future educational arrangements for the new school. Mr Pickup, innovative as ever, had devised his own means of overcoming the tedium surrounding the winding-up of Parkland Community High, as the Simpson diaries for April will explain.

Monday

Much discussion this morning about next Friday's meeting with the staff of Rockston High, with which school we are due to merge next session. Mr Pickup has opened a book on the chances of Parkland High's staff members retaining their respective jobs after the event. Apparently, Mr Major – our somewhat lethargic assistant head – is odds-on favourite to go and consequently heads Mr Pickup's list of 'Teachers For The Chop', which compilation he insensitively chalked on a blackboard in his RE base this morning. Surprisingly close in the betting stakes was the expected departure of our head teacher, Mr Ross:

'Oh yes,' explained Pickup in response to my exclamation of surprise at finding such short odds on the rectorial employment prospects. 'He would've been even shorter, but there's been no definite news about his early retirment application yet.'

'Early retirement?' I queried. 'Mr Ross? But he's only 52, and he told me just last week how immensely he was looking forward to the challenge of starting afresh with a new school, what with –'

'Did he now?' Pickup raised a contemplative eyebrow before pursing his lips, picking up a duster and chalk, and swiftly amending the stakes on Mr Ross's departure from 5/1 to 3/1. 'That just about settles it, then. He's obviously getting ready to go ...'

Tuesday

Martin Pratt, our pony-tailed history supply teacher, has abandoned any pretence of hoping to remain in a full-time professorial appointment by abandoning his registration on the supply-list. He has been apparently wearied by the demands of lesson preparation which have been thrust upon him since he was asked to teach history classes instead of sit at the front of the classroom reading newspapers.

His subsequent announcement that he was going to take some 'paternity leave' in order to look after the newly-born infant which he and his wife Fiona have just produced was nevertheless met with a degree of incredulity by most of the staff, myself included.

'But what'll they do for *money*?' I asked Mr Pickup at morning interval, only to be informed that – between Fiona's maternity payments, and the unemployment benefit to which Martin would soon be entitled – they should find things bearable.

'And then there's Martin's job at the pub, of course,' he added. '– should be able to go almost full-time on that, I'd imagine ...'

'Ah-ha,' I corrected him. 'Not if he's signing on as unemployed, remember?'

Pickup looked scornfully across the coffee table. 'Are you joking, Simpson?' he enquired archly before rubbing thumb and forefinger together in avaricious impersonation. 'Every penny counts for the Pratts of this world, you know. Screw the authorities for everything you can get – and then keep on screwing that little bit more.'

'I'm sorry, Mr Pickup,' I contradicted him. 'I know I don't like him, but I don't think even Martin Pratt would stoop to such levels of deception.'

'Hah!' he exclaimed. 'Don't you believe it! Honestly, Simpson, it's time you –'

'I'm sorry,' I excused myself before getting involved in another of Pickup's little homilies. 'I'll have to go and do some guidance work: I've got an important interview with Alan McLeary's parents on Thursday, and I want to make sure I've gathered all the written evidence about their son's disgraceful behaviour before they arrive – especially after last month's arson attack at Hollydown hen-house.'

'McLeary's parents?' Pickup restrained me momentarily. 'You've actually got *them* to come and see *you*?'

'Well, yes, sort of,' I smiled modestly.

'What d'you mean, sort of?' he jumped in suspiciously. 'They've never been inside this school since the day their son came into first year – not even when the boss summonsed them to explain why the little bastard'd gassed the biology department's hamsters. How on earth have you managed to persuade them to come in?'

'Well, actually,' I confessed. 'I didn't. It was they who wanted to see *me* about something –' Pickup looked aghast, but I hurried on '– so I'm going to take the opportunity to discuss the pastoral relationships which I'm keen to engender among Alan's year-group, and how I won't tolerate his anti-social behaviour any longer.'

'Morris,' Mr Pickup laid an avuncular hand on my shoulder. 'If McLeary's mother and father have asked to see *you*, then it means only one thing: they're not coming in to discuss how *they* can help the school overcome their son's anti-social tendencies.'

'No?' I questioned.

'No. It means they're in to make a *complaint* about something.'

'Oh really?'

'Yes, really! That's the only reason parents like that ever set foot across the school threshold. And if I were you I'd find out quickly what they're in to complain about before you get ready to dish out a litany of their dear offspring's misdemeanours. Forewarned is forearmed, y'know.'

I thanked him for the advice and suggested I would be able to deal perfectly competently with any such case of parental dissatisfaction which McLeary's parents might, or might not, want to raise.

Wednesday

Mr Pickup was right about Mr & Mrs McLeary. I discovered this morning that Monica Cunningham had given Alan a row for swearing repeatedly in her computing class last week; McLeary, of course, had denied the charge and the resultant discussion between them had concluded with McLeary's promise of parental retribution in the form of a familial visit .

To be perfectly honest, I don't think it matters *why* they're coming to see me: I fully intend our meeting to concentrate entirely on their son's appalling disciplinary record at the school, and look forward to acquainting them with the facts tomorrow.

Meanwhile, Mr Pickup's betting blackboard has had an addition to the frame of 'Teachers For The Chop': actually, I think it's his little joke, because he's added the name of Richard Dick as a 100/1 outsider, despite the fact that everyone in the staff is only too well aware of our dynamic assistant head's ambitious intentions of attaining even greater prominence at the new school.

Such ambitions became even more patently obvious this morning when he entered the staffroom carrying an extra briefcase. It was George Crumley, our slightly irascible principal teacher of geography, who first challenged him about the extra load.

'Looking after someone else's briefcase as well as your own, Dick?' he queried.

'No, no,' Mr Dick replied, '– it's just that –' he broke off with apparent embarrassment, although with evident secret delight that someone had noticed the extra briefcase.

'Well, it's just,' he oozed quickly on, 'that I seem to find myself with so much extra work these days that I'm having to bring in two briefcases instead of the usual one.'

George was speechless – as indeed were the rest of us listening in – as Mr Dick outlined the plethora of reports he was having to deal with at present, the combination of whose paperwork had given him cause for the extra briefcase:

'Quite honestly, between the implementation of these team-building exercises and the merger reports,' – he held up one brief-case – 'plus the anti-racism guidelines, 5–14 implementation and appraisal policy in this one,' – he held up the other – 'sometimes I just don't know where I'm going to find the time for it all.'

'Yes,' replied George Crumley drily. 'It's just as well you never see any children in the course of your working day, isn't it? That would *really* bugger up your timetable, I suppose.' With which he turned on his heel and left Dick alone with his briefcases.

Thursday

An unnerving interview with Mr & Mrs McLeary. Despite my attempts to acquaint them with the more lurid details of Alan's recent behaviour, they were prepared only to discuss the alleged slight which had been cast on their son's integrity by Monica Cunningham.

'Naw!' bellowed Mr McLeary as I endeavoured to explain my viewpoint on swearing at teachers. '*You* listen tae *me*, four-eyes! Ah'm no' sayin' ma son's perfect, no' by any manner o' means,' – to which statement I could only nod vigorous assent before he continued – 'but whit ah *am* sayin' is that no way – no fuckin' *way* –' he jabbed a forceful finger at me, 'would ma' boy ever swerr in fronty a teacher. Wur respoansible parents, Mr Simpson, an' me an' his mammy ur real *strict* about swerrin' – so if ye just lead me tae that wee Cunningham bitch, then we'll see who's tellin' the bloody truth. Am ah right, Senga?' he folded his arms incontro-vertibly upon the table.

Mrs McLeary seemed to realise that his question was a rhetori-cal one, for she drifted into a wandering and misty-eyed mono-logue concerning her son's attributes, which list concluded with

the unlikely statement that McLeary Junior was 'just a wee treasure.'

Commendably restraining myself from the obvious enquiry about the location from which she had therefore dug him up, I managed to conclude the interview by suggesting that I would discuss the matter with Mrs Cunningham myself before arranging a joint meeting of the parties. Mr McLeary didn't seem very enthusiastic, indicating instead that he 'wanted tae see some bloody action', but Mrs McLeary managed to persuade him that they could leave it for the moment lest she miss her afternoon bingo session.

I certainly feel that I'm earning my responsibility allowance these days.

Friday

A difficult day. I suggested to Monica Cunningham that the verbal reprimand which she had issued to Alan McLeary over the question of his abusive language might need to be explained in a little more detail to the boy's father. Unfortunately, she's recently been on an assertiveness course, and reconciliation seemed the farthest thing from her mind.

'What!' she barked across the coffee table at morning break. 'If there's any explaining to do, Morris, it'd better come from that sub-literate child as to why he finds it necessary to punctuate every second sentence with a string of obscenities that would make a trooper blush! Mind you,' she added reflectively, 'if all I hear of his father's true, then it's no wonder the boy's vocabulary's as limited as it is.'

I suppose she has a point, but I have to say she's not making my own job any easier; sadly, her analysis of the situation was not shared by Mr McLeary, who this morning made a severe nuisance of himself with Mr Tod, demanding to see 'the wee cow who'd picked oan Alan.' Tod was understandably irritated to be accosted by a man whom he later described as 'a walking swear-box':

'Honestly. Simpson – why couldn't you deal with this yourself?' he complained to me at lunchtime

'But I did,' I pleaded earnestly.

'Oh?' replied Tod tartly. 'Not according to Mr McLeary you didn't. Said he'd got no satisfaction from you whatsoever and that as far as guidance was concerned you – and I paraphrase slightly – "couldn't guide a pensioner to an effing bus-stop". Hardly seem to have inspired confidence in the man, Simpson. Eh?'

I muttered something about a right of reply but he looked sceptical, so I excused myself lest I miss my lift to Rockston for the afternoon in-service meeting of our pre-merger staffs.

It was a brief, joyless affair – both sets of teachers sat on opposite sides of the stark lecture theatre where the meeting was held and spoke hardly a word to each other throughout the entire meeting. Frankly, it all seemed a bit pointless: both headmasters spoke at great length about the 'dynamic educational challenges about to be presented to us in setting up a new school from scratch' – at the same time as they were explaining their respective sorrows that neither of them would be able to take part in these challenges owing to their joint success in gaining early retirement as of next session.

'So you were right,' I congratulated Pickup in The Rockston Arms after 4 o'clock. 'Mr Ross *is* for the off – and Mr Blake as well?'

'Mmm,' mused Pickup as he ordered another drink (from Martin Pratt, incidentally, to my extreme indignation). 'And where d'you think that leaves us for a new headteacher, Simpson?'

'Maybe you should open another book?' I joked with him.

'I have,' he nodded seriously. 'Tod's the odds-on favourite for the headship, but it'll be a close-run thing for the new depute between old Jamie Wilson at Rockston or Tricky-Dicky, the Young Pretender.'

'Oh, give it a rest,' I punched him playfully, before a sudden thought came to mind.

'Um ... incidentally –' I hesitated in my enquiry, but Pickup merely raised his eyebrows in innocence. 'See that first book you opened, on "Teachers For The Chop"?'

'Yes,' Pickup intoned gravely.

'Uh – whereabouts – um – my own – well I just wondered – uh ...?'

'Yourself?' Pickup eventually put me out of my misery. 'My dear boy,' he laughed before summing up the educational catastrophes of my career to date, with particular reference to the arson, abuse and practical jokes perpetrated by my guidance group in the last eight weeks, for all of which actions I seem to be unfairly held responsible by the senior management team.

'Sorry, Morris' he sighed apologetically. 'I'm not taking any more bets on you, I'm afraid – the compulsory transfer's too much of a certainty to my mind.'

With which insolicitous, comfortless advice, he laughed loud, patted me on the back and asked me to get the next round as Pratt came scurrying over for our order.

'Yes gents? What'll it be?' he smirked with insolence.

'Ohh – bb ... bb ...,' my lips hardened and my temper rose in frustration with Pickup. 'Bb ... Buy your own!' I broke out in a rare display of temper before turning on my heel and leaving Pickup alone at the bar. Too much of a certainty indeed!

May

As well as the tension caused by Mr Pickup's sarcastic remarks in the Pig and Whistle, Morris also had the possible return of Frank Parker to worry about. Even if he *was* to remain in the newly-merged school, Morris reasoned, there was no guarantee of retaining his APT guidance job – and its accompanying responsibility allowance – once Mr Parker returned from his secondment. Also, of course, there was his opposite number – the current APT guidance at Rockston – to be considered.

Of course, other members of staff were planning for the future as well, none more so than Mr Ross, for whom the prospect of early retirement was a source of endless and euphoric conjecture. His successor was due to be announced in May, but apart from the hierarchical deliberations surrounding this appointment, the school had to carry on as if everything were normal.

At least, for once, a cessation had been called to the normal hostilities between the geography and history departments at this time of year. Morris recalled with amused dismay the previous battles between George Crumley and Martin Henderson to provide the most attractive diet of field trips for pupils in second year, all designed to attract a greater proportion of the year group to their respective subjects when it came to choosing options for study in the third year. However, given the abnormal circumstances surrounding the school's future status, both Henderson and Crumley had agreed to a temporary truce by calling off their respective field trips for this year. That, at least, was Morris's understanding of the situation – until he met with Martin Henderson one Monday in May.

Before speaking to Henderson, however, he had been in receipt of some very good news on the job front …

Monday

Mr Pickup's gloomy prognosis about my future employment prospects at our soon-to-merge school look to be completely unfounded, with the news today that my opposite number, the APT guidance at Rockston High, is set to emigrate for a teaching job in Malawi. Even Pickup accepted that my chances looked rosier than hitherto:

'And I doubt if we'll ever see Frank Parker again,' he confided to me this afternoon, in reference to the APT guidance for whom I am currently 'acting-up' at Parkland High. Parker is still on secondment to an office-based guidance project reporting on social interactivity within neighbourhood areas of priority treatment.

'No?' I queried eagerly. 'Why not?'

'Morris,' he explained patiently: 'Frank Parker's been out of school for a year now. He's tasted freedom. He's tasted life without 30 screaming children at his feet every hour of the day. And once he's done that, there's no way he'll want to come back to a dump like –'

'But surely his secondment's due to finish this month?' I countered. 'He'll *have* to come back by the end of term, and where does that leave me?'

'It leaves you exactly where you are,' he repeated. 'Just because his secondment's finished doesn't mean Frank Parker won't persuade them to extend it for another twelve months – or even devise a permanent post because he's suddenly convinced them that he's indispensable along there, churning out report after report on guidance procedures and initiatives, without ever actually having to go near a maladjusted child in the course of his working day.'

'So you think I might actually get his job full time?' my eyes opened wide with anticipation.

'Why not?' shrugged Pickup. 'You're no more useless than the rest of the guidance staff in this place.'

I thanked him coolly for the expression of confidence, and scurried off to ask Mr Ross if he'd heard anything from Frank Parker recently. Unfortunately, he's away until Wednesday on a management course for headteachers – rather pointless, I feel, given his imminent retirement – so I'll have to wait until he returns

Meanwhile, Martin Henderson had apparently been looking for me with a request that I help out with Friday's history field trip to the local museum with 18 second-year pupils: the lack of a proper supply teacher in the department had meant he was short of an extra pair of supervisory hands, and – having eventually found me – he pointed out that I did have a morning devoid of class contact, so could I help out?

'Certainly, Martin,' I was happy to accede. 'But I didn't think you were *having* any field trips this year?'

He looked secretive. 'Um. Well we weren't. But we are now,' he admitted furtively. 'I reckoned it was unfair to deprive the kids of the curricular enhancement they'd normally get from that kind of thing. But I'd be grateful,' he added quietly, 'if you didn't mention it to the geography department until it's all set up. OK?'

It seemed a strange request, but he insisted; so I agreed.

Tuesday

Mr Ross turned up at school this morning after all: apparently, he himself had fallen to reflection upon the wisdom of attending a course for headteachers only four weeks prior to retirement and – having refused to take part in a psychological role-play activity which had required him to enact a 'confrontational situation with a member of his senior management team' – he had decided to come back to school instead of attending the second day of the course.

'What was the bloody point?' he had apparently queried our depute Mr Tod this morning. 'I can enact a confrontational situation for real with you bastards any day of the week!' With which he had laughed out loud, slapped Tod on the back, and disappeared into his office.

'He's demob happy,' diagnosed Mr Tod as he related the story at morning break. 'Can't say I blame him, really.'

I sensed a window of opportunity to enquire about Frank Parker's secondment, so hurried away to see Mr Ross immediately. I confess to a degree of surprise upon finding him in a relaxed, almost somnolent position, feet across his desk, and casually scanning a copy of *101 Ideas For Your Retirement* .

'Uh – Mr Ross?' I queried tentatively. 'Could I see you for a moment please?'

'Um – sorry, Mr Simpson,' he pushed a secretive finger to his mouth. 'Ssh – I'm not actually here today.'

'Sorry?' I queried.

'I'm not actually here today,' he repeated softly. 'I'm on a course. I'm back tomorrow, so perhaps you could come and see me then?'

'But you *are* here,' I politely pointed out. 'So couldn't we – ?'

'No, I'm sorry, Mr Simpson,' he insisted calmly. 'I'm afraid I'm *not* actually here, as I'm sure you'll realise if you consult the school diary. But I'll happily see you tomorrow, when I *am* here.'

'Um – thank-you,' I decided to admit defeat, faced with such irrefutable – if impenetrable – logic. 'Thank you very much, Mr Ross.' Having resolved to make my enquiry of someone closer to sanity, I went back to the staffroom in search of Mr Tod. Perhaps it's as well that Mr Ross is due to retire soon. I wonder who'll be our new rector?

Wednesday

The succession has been announced! Mr Tod has been appointed headteacher of the newly-merged school, while Mr Dick has attained the giddy heights of his depute.

Our new rector seemed to take the news fairly in his stride, but I have rarely seen anyone so excited as Richard Dick. He arrived in school this morning with his usual complement of two briefcases, plus an extra folder of documentation under his arm, preparatory paperwork for a meeting with Mr Tod on possible names for the new school.

'Gosh,' he preened, anxiously awaiting the congratulatory remarks of his colleagues. 'I don't know where I'm going to find time for everything today, what with having to see Mr Tod about a name for the new school, plus finishing off that report on our multi-cultural policies.' He paused for breath and smiled warmly around the staffroom.

Thirty pairs of eyes bored into him, and thirty mouths resolutely refused to offer any form of congratulatory remark. Except mine.

'Well done, Dick,' I offered the hand of friendship. 'It's been –' I started to speak, but he needed no further opportunity.

'Gosh thanks, Morris,' he enthused with indecent haste. 'You know, I wasn't sure whether I'd get it or not, but it's really been a tremendous boost, and I know I can hardly *wait* to get started! I really feel that it's a wonderful challenge for us all, don't you? The chance to begin afresh, the chance to provide a much more balanced curriculum, and of course the chance to develop a more interactive style of school management as well. So many new chances!' he enthused earnestly.

I thought I sensed an echo of a carefully prepared interview speech, but kept my own counsel on the matter. Not so Mr Pickup: suddenly, he thrust both forefingers into his mouth, made a series of vomiting noises, and entered the gents' toilet. As the door shut behind him, he called out in loud imitation of our newly appointed depute:

'And what about the chance to have a bloody huge salary increase as well? Don't forget that one, sunshine!'

Mr Dick looked down at the floor, clearly embarrassed at Pickup's outburst. Looking up again, he quickly regained his composure.

'Good,' he smiled wanly. 'That's just the kind of outspoken comment I'm more than happy to receive. That's what management's all about, you know. Any problems, any complaints, any criticisms – just bring them to me. That's what I'm here for.'

Upon which, he hastily scurried away lest anyone take him up on the offer.

Thursday

A one-person deputation awaited my arrival at school this morning, in the person of George Crumley, principal teacher of geography.

'Simpson!' he greeted me angrily. 'What the hell's this about your helping out with the second-year history field-trip?'

Bewildered by his tone, I admitted the charge and asked if he had anything to complain about.

'Of course I've got something to complain about!' he exclaimed. 'I had an unwritten agreement with Martin Henderson that we'd both forget about field-trips this year. And now he tells me that you've gone behind my back to help him arrange one after all. Bloody Judas!' he swore at me before striding away, leaving me confused and concerned.

As ever, it was left to Pickup to explain George's discomfiture at morning break:

'It's the options again, Morris,' he reminded me of the constant battle between the social subjects to attain pre-eminence in the second year option sheet for future areas of study; or, as he so quaintly put it: 'It's all about bums on seats in the third year.'

'So for the past 15 years,' he elaborated, 'the history and geography departments have been slogging it out trying to arrange the most attractive field-trips to ensure the litle darlings make the right selection in Column 4. Except for once they'd called a truce,' he went on. 'What with the school roll down to 210, and a whole new batch of kids in Rockston that they couldn't get their claws into, George and Martin agreed to give themselves a rest this year. But,' he narrowed his eyes in admiration, 'Martin's obviously worked a flanker.'

'Oh, that's ridiculous!' I complained. 'These trips are simply an opportunity to offer an enhancement of the curriculum, no matter *which* department takes them. And to suggest that Martin and George are engaged in some kind of petty rivalry to offer the best field trip to persuade pupils that – well it's quite ridiculous,' I repeated. 'Remember, Pickup, these are grown men we're talking about.'

'I know,' he shook his head regretfully. 'That's what makes it all the more pathetic, really.'

Friday

Sadly, the museum trip proved to be something of an educational anti-climax.

To be fair to Martin Henderson, it wasn't his fault: he had prepared a host of informative worksheets before the visit, and had even involved the class in a series of historical roleplays to bring some verisimilitude to the visit. Similarly, the museum's education officer had provided a highly illustrated workbook for each child to record details of primary source material from the museum's wide and varied collection of displays.

Alas, however, the only topic of any interest whatsoever to the pupils was the whereabouts of the museum shop. As soon as the bus disgorged its load at the museum entrance, the cry went up:

'Sur! Werr's the shoap? Wit kin ye buy?'

Martin valiantly insisted that the pupils complete their worksheets before attempting to purchase any souvenirs of the visit: a frantic dash around fourteen rooms (average time per pupil: 35 seconds in each room) allowed most of them to append a series of ticks to the various multi-choice questions on offer as well as copy the occasional word from a display case to fill in a few blanks on their respective sheets.

Thereafter, the entire contingent insisted upon spending the next 40 minutes milling around the museum's souvenir shop. After the fourth case of attempted shoplifting, the sales assistant sensibly decreed that only three pupils be allowed in at any one time, which restriction led to severe disciplinary problems in the hallway outside the shop. So much for curricular enhancement, I thought to myself.

Eventually, having purchased a veritable cornucopia of plastic stickers, badges, coloured pencils and rubbers, the majority of pupils settled themselves on the floor and coloured in some worksheets. Perhaps naïvely, I wondered aloud whether they couldn't have performed such an exercise within the confines of their school classroom. Martin smiled enigmatically, suggested that this was a 'different kind of learning experience' and that we should 'let them experience the joys of living history'.

Privately, I began to suspect that Pickup's assessment had been correct, a suspicion that was confirmed during the return bus journey.

'Well, then,' Martin enquired of Damian Taylor. 'Enjoy that, did you?'

'Oh aye, sur,' replied Damian.

'Thinking of taking history next year, then?' Martin enquired – just a little too eagerly, I couldn't help but wonder.

'Uh – dunno, sur,' Damian lounged back in his seat. 'No' shoor yet. Ahm waitin' till aftur the geography trip.'

'What?' Martin Henderson nearly jumped down the boy's throat. '*What* geography trip?'

'Mr Crumley's geography trip,' replied Damian. 'Wur gaun tae the seaside furra cupply days,' he explained patiently. '– lookin' at river basin furmations.'

Martin Henderson stiffened percepibly. 'Two days at the sea side? River basin formations?' he queried, incredulous with rage.

'Aye, sur,' confirmed Damian. 'Mr Crumley telt us about it yesturday.'

'Did he now?' muttered Henderson, clearly furious at this new development. Mouth firmly set, he gazed into the middle distance and fell to solitary reflection.

'Bastard ...' he whispered quietly to himself. 'Sneaky little bastard.'

'Sorry, sur?' queried Damian. 'D'ye say somethin'?'

'Ha-hah!' laughed Henderson, suddenly alert again. 'Not at all, Damian. Sorry.'

Personally, I considered his remark extremely unprofessional, but I thought it better to refrain from comment. One look at Martin Henderson's twisted and embittered countenance swiftly convinced me that this was one of my wiser decisions.

June

The omens for a happy merger of Parkland Community High with Rockston High were not auspicious. Firstly, there was the fact that neither school enjoyed an enviable reputation, in either academic or sociological terms. And, even at this late stage in the proceedings, it didn't look as if the two sets of staff were likely to blend in the harmonious manner necessary for the smooth and uninterrupted education of their combined sets of pupils.

The Rockston staff, in particular, had been infuriated by the promoted post appointments which were in the making: as had been the case with previous regional mergers of schools, the staff who were perceived as having 'lost' their school building – in this case Parkland's – were tending to be in receipt of nearly all posts of elevation in the new school. Possibly this was in recognition of their greater academic stature – although such an interpretation would seem unlikely to any objective observer; alternatively, it was possible that such a policy (unwritten, of course) could be seen as a compensatory gesture for the upheaval required of those teachers who were leaving Parkland.

Needless to say, Pickup's gambling enthusiasms discovered yet another avenue of opportunity in such a situation. Fortunately, few – if any – of the Rockston staff got to hear of his nefarious activities: the act of laying yet further wagers on future employment prospects for certain of their teaching staff could well have been viewed as an inflammatory gesture. By the time the schools actually merged, however, it would all have been forgotten about, because the last days of Parkland High were to prove inflammatory in other, more tangible, respects.

Thus – for reasons which will become obvious – it was with a heaviness of heart that Morris Simpson composed his diary for the end of June, destined to be the last – and historic – such entry from Parkland High School.

Monday

This is the last full week of existence for Parkland Community High School. The end of session sees us close our doors to pupils for the last time before we officially merge with our neighbouring school, Rockston High.

There has been a lot of bitterness from the Rockston staff over recent appointments of promoted staff in the new school. The most senior positions having been announced last month, the procedure is now 'trickling down to the poor bloody infantry', as Mr Pickup put it this morning. In what is being seen as blatantly positive discrimination in favour of the school staff who are losing their own building, 11 of the 14 principal teacher posts so far allocated have been awarded to ex-Parkland staff, with only the result of the English PT post yet to be announced.

Pickup – who tells me he has taken out an extremely adventurous wager on the eventual likely total of Parkland winners – has a further particularly vested interest in that he is due to hear tomorrow of his own fate with regard to the post of assistant principal teacher in charge of religious education. For my own part, I've been delighted to discover that – in line with Pickup's predictions last month – my acting APT guidance post looks set to be made permanent and, with my opposite number at Rockston due to leave the country, I am almost certain to be returned unopposed.

Pickup has made a number of snide comments about my having achieved such dizzy promotional heights 'through the back door', as he puts it, but I have refused to be goaded by his remarks. Merit will out, I always feel.

Tuesday

Pickup has got the assistant principal's job in RE. Apparently, his own opposite number at Rockston has decided to opt for early retirement on the grounds of curricular despair, leaving the field wide open for Pickup. Of course, I took the chance to get my own back with a few comments about back-door promotion, but he wasn't really listening. In fact, he seemed almost disinterested in his own success, preferring instead to speak at length with Simon Young, my own (acting) principal teacher of English, whose interview for the new school's PT post is tomorrow. Indeed, Pickup appeared more concerned about the outcome of this appointment than his own – I wonder if it's anything to do with the wager he's taken out?

'So how d'you reckon your chances, Simon?' he enquired solicitously.

'Oh, I dunno,' Simon sighed wearily. 'I'm honestly not even sure that I *want* the ruddy job, to be honest with you.'

Pickup nearly jumped down his throat. 'What?' he grabbed Simon by the arm. 'Don't say that, Simon!' he gasped fiercely. 'You can't mean it?' he pleaded.

Simon looked surprised. 'Come off it,' he prised Pickup's fingers gently from his forearm. 'Of course I can mean it. Quite frankly, after 39 months as acting PT I think I've seen enough of the job to realise the extra money's probably not worth it. Really Pickup, I'd be perfectly happy returning to my old APT post.'

Pickup looked aghast, his face drained of colour. 'Um ... eh ...' he seemed at a complete loss for words and shook his head in bewilderment before pulling himself together to suggest his usual solution at moments of crisis:

'Look – uh – listen, Simon,' he confided secretively. 'What d'you say to a few quick ones after school, eh? Down the Pig and Whistle? Just you and me? Eh?'

I wonder what he's hatching.

Retiral dinner in the Parkland Arms tomorrow evening to mark the respective departures of Messrs Ross and Major.

Before that, however, much debate continues to take place over the likely name for our newly-merged school: Mr Tod, our rector-in-waiting, has been in several conference sessions with Richard Dick (the new depute) and other members of the senior management team, but they have yet to emerge with any concrete decision. The status quo is not tenable, of course, lest anyone feel that Rockston High has 'taken over' Parkland High, or vice-versa if the school were to retain its Parkland High appellation. My most recent information is that 'Rockston Academy' is the front-runner at present, but debate has apparently been torrid, some contributors to the discussion feeling that 'Parkland Grammar' would be a more appropriate draw for any parents gullible enough to believe the implications of such a name.

'Oh, it makes me bloody sick!' swore Pickup when I outlined the latest news at lunchtime.

'Sorry?' I started in surprise.

'All this pretentious, quasi-academic crap they're coming up with. Here they are, lumping two of the worst schools in the region together and trying to pretend that we're suddenly going to provide the district with an academic strike-rate that'll put bloody Eton in the shade! Who do they think they're fooling, Morris? Tell me that!'

I began to take him severely to task over such demotivating remarks, pointing out that if teachers at the new school – especially assistant principal teachers like ourselves – let such attitudes be made public, then we would be guilty of providing a self-fulfilling prophecy.

Indeed, I was just getting into my stride when Simon Young walked into the room. Pickup immediately abandoned any pretence of listening to what I was saying and jumped to his feet.

'Well?' he questioned breathlessly. 'How did it go? Did you get it, Simon? Did you?'

Provocatively, Simon raised a secretive eyebrow, put a finger to his nose – and then broke into a broad grin before announcing that, yes, in view of the fact that his opposite number at Rockston had less experience than Simon (he had apparently only been 24 months acting as principal teacher as opposed to Simon's 39), then he, Simon Young, had just been appointed permanent principal teacher of English at Rockston Grammar, or Parkland

Academy, or whatever the new school was to be called.

I was just getting to my feet to give him a congratulatory shake of the hand when Pickup raised both arms in the air, shouted 'BINGO!' at the very top of his voice before barging past – rudely elbowing me back into my seat as he did so – and launching himself at Simon Young with an impassioned and all encircling bear-hug.

'Ya wee beauty!' he shouted once more, before adding, *sotto voce*: 'I'll see you all right for your cut, Simon, OK? Praise be!' he concluded, growing louder once more, and lifting his eyes heavenwards in divinely-directed gratitude. 'Thank-you, God. Oh thank-you so much,' he squeaked in child-like excitement.

Actually, I'd never thought of Pickup as a religious man – especially given the subject he teaches – but once he'd calmed down and allowed Simon out of his affectionate embrace, all was revealed: apparently, something which Pickup calls a treble accumulator had seen him accurately predict both of the head and depute posts in our new school plus the eventual total of 12 new principal teachers to be appointed from the staff of Parkland High. Simon's appointment had been the final piece in his gambling jigsaw, hence the obvious subject of their intimate conversation in the Pig and Whistle last night. I refrained from enquiring about Simon's promised share of the proceeds, but was intrigued to learn that Pickup's resultant winnings will probably (he informed me confidentially) keep him in beer money for the next two years.

In which case it must be an enormous sum, that's all I can say. Personally, I feel it to be highly unprofessional, betting on such an issue – next thing you know, we'll have parents and teachers betting on their pupils' examination results!

Thursday

The school being almost entirely devoid of pupils in these concluding days of term, I have been able to get on with much clearing out of my classroom prior to the Rockston move next week. In many respects it has been a very emotional exercise, scouring the memories of my seven-year career here. Old registers and mark books brought back a host of recollections, and I even came across one of the essays which Rose McShane – a former pupil of some notoriety – had presented in supreme effort for her (third repeat) O grade preliminary examination some three years ago now.

Its total length of four lines and three words (for a mark out of 30, if I remember rightly) reminded me of the endless torments to which I found myself subject in attempting to deal with one of the worst-behaved and illiterate pupils it's ever been my misfortune to have to try and teach. I can only hope I won't come across anyone like *her* in the new school!

Aside from clearing most of this rubbish out, I've at last completed the cataloguing of my guidance records as well as my departmental lesson-plans: Mr Tod had actually asked for all such records to be transferred to Rockston by yesterday afternoon, but I don't know where he imagines we'd all have found the time to do so. At least, having gathered all the material together, I was able to fill three large boxes on my desk prior to moving it out; however, due to this evening's retirement dinner, I had to postpone the actual removal until tomorrow, when I have some free time.

The retirement dinner itself was unbelievably tedious, enlivened only by the fact that I managed to locate myself next to David Pickup for the evening. Aside from the usual geniality of his company, I confess to being attracted by the liberality with which he was dispensing complimentary rounds of drinks to anyone prepared to listen long enough to his umpteenth repetition of the mathematical odds which he had overcome in his recent bookmaking triumph.

Otherwise, the evening was marked by indifferent catering and an endless round of laudatory speeches which made me begin to wonder if I was at the right function, so sycophantic were some of the comments made about the retirees. To hear, for example, John Ross described by the divisional education officer as a 'colossus of education whose devotion to duty and to children knew no limits' was a bit thick. The two of them have hated the sight of each other ever since Ross took up post.

Mr Ross himself gave a speech which outlasted any other, even given its premature conclusion. He began by saying that 'it didn't seem like 27 years since he had started his career in education'. By the end of his 'brief remarks' (his phrase, not mine), it seemed to me like a damned sight *longer* than 27 years! Indeed, he'd probably still be speaking now if Pickup hadn't stood up, belched loudly, and blown a party hooter to announce 'Free drinks at the bar all round!' The resultant rugby-scrum effectively concluded Mr Ross's speech for him, and just as well. It was a sad end to an inglorious career.

Friday

Alas, an even sadder conclusion to the term awaited my arrival at school this morning. I first realised something was amiss when I had to leave the bus before my usual stop, owing to the closure of Parkland Crescent. A large gathering of pupils, staff and onlookers, plus the presence of several fire-fighting appliances and a veritable profusion of water-hoses across the street soon alerted me to the fact that a fairly major conflagration had occurred overnight.

Indeed, this proved to be the case, and further investigation revealed that the fire in question had ensured the almost complete destruction of Parkland Community High School. Acrid smoke still rose from the charred and blackened shell of the entire main building, and even the portable huts on the outer edge of the school had been utterly consumed.

I sought out Mr Pickup, standing on the fringes of the crowd and shaking his head sorrowfully. 'Good heavens!' I gasped, shocked at the devastation. 'It's a good thing this didn't happen when there were any pupils in the building, isn't it?'

Pickup looked witheringly down at me, shook his head, and

explained his own interpretation of the proceedings.

'Yes,' he said drily, 'Although I hardly think they're likely to set light to the place when they're inside it, Simpson. Not even *our* pupils are that stupid!'

'You what?' I queried, shocked. 'Surely you can't mean –'

'Oh, of course I mean!' he snapped back at me. 'Usual story, Simpson. There's arson about, as if you couldn't work it out for yourself – and maybe we should be grateful for it: the little buggers know full well the place is closing down, and they know full well it'll be left to lie derelict by the education department for the next umpteen years, so they'd have been going to torch it in the very near future anyway. At least they waited till the end of term – or near it, at any rate – to take matters into their own hands.'

'Mmm,' agreed Mr Tod, who had chanced to overhear Pickup's assessment of the situation. 'Think you're probably right, Pickup,' he agreed, before congratulating himself on the foresight of his administrative organisation. 'And at least we've got all the school records out before the place went up,' he commented, sending a chill into the pit of my stomach. 'Good job that's all done.'

'Yes,' Pickup agreed thoughtfully. 'Not much chance of salvaging anything out of that lot – eh, Morris?' he gestured expansively across the scene of desolation.

'Uh – no,' I gulped, my mouth suddenly as ashen as the smouldering remains in front of us, my mind's eye fixed entirely on a vision of three large cardboard boxes containing guidance records, last seen on the table in my guidance office, and now completely razed to the ground.

Hastily, I excused myself on the pretext of a smoke-induced coughing fit. Mr Tod looked on with concern as I staggered away, but I hadn't the heart to tell him the truth. Or the courage.

August

The matter of the destroyed guidance records was a source of serious concern to Morris over the summer holidays, but he attempted to put them out of his mind as he embarked upon a two-week cycling tour towards the end of July.

This holiday was to provide a chance for the Simpson mental batteries to be recharged: it had been a limp and dispiriting session in so many ways, and Morris felt he needed the break to reflect upon the forthcoming term. Ultimately, despite his initial despair at losing a complete set of lesson-plans as well as the guidance records, he persuaded himself that the fire which had so effectively wiped out all remnants of his teaching career to date could be looked upon as a blessing in disguise. This, Morris thought to himself as he cycled down many a country lane, would be an opportunity to make a personal fresh start, to cleanse himself of old ideas and inject a new sense of passion, urgency and commitment to his educational endeavours.

Would that others had felt so enthusiastic. Mr Pickup, needless to say, refused to allow any thought or consideration of school life to cross his mind throughout the six week summer break, an approach which was shared by the vast majority of his colleagues. And even the regional authority seemed to have forgotten about their newly-merged school: upon his return from the cycling tour, Morris scanned back numbers of the local papers for any outcome on the school's new name, yet a decision still appeared unforthcoming. To many of the staff – Mr Dick excepted, perhaps – the matter of the new school's name was completely immaterial; to Morris, it was a matter of profound educational anticipation.

Fortunately – and to the surprise of many – a decision had been taken by the opening day of term.

Monday: First In-Service Day

A new term. And a new school. And, after many months of deliberation, a new name as well.

Having taken the best part of nineteen weeks arguing over the possible appelations for our newly merged Parkland and Rockston Community High Schools, the regional council and school senior management team have finally decided upon the name of Greenfield Academy. Of course, the first I learned of it – as a mere teacher in the place – was the erection of a spanking new metallic sign outside the gates when I reported for duty first thing this morning.

'So then, Mr Pickup,' I greeted my religious education colleague as we snatched a quick cup of coffee before the inaugural staff meeting. 'What d'you think of the new name?'

'Hah!' he scoffed. 'Like I said last term, Simpson: pretentious semi-academic crap, that's all. Here we are at the end of Ashvale Crescent, so what's our logical name? Ashvale Comprehensive,' he answered himself immediately with conviction, and no little sarcasm in his voice. 'But no. Ashvale Comprehensive doesn't sound *nearly* as attractive as Greenfield Academy to any aspiring parent, does it? Yet the nearest we get to any green fields in this glorified cesspit of a school is if you stick your head out the C floor girls' toilets and crane your neck to the east: I think you'll see a green field in the distance then ...' he tailed off in cynical reflection.

I resisted the temptation to ask how Pickup could recall with such clarity the view from the C floor girls' toilets and instead put forward my suggestion that the educational connotations of being an Academy would be more likely to act as a magnet to those aspiring parents of the pupils we were keenest to attract to the school.

'Precisely!' he confirmed eagerly. 'But just think what a bloody disappointment's going to greet them once their kids have been in the place for a fortnight! Theyll be high-tailing it out the front door faster than you can say "Parents' Charter"!'

I hardly think Pickup's attitude is to be commended. Personally, I view the opening of our new school as an exciting challenge, a chance to learn from our previous mistakes and start afresh with a clean slate. And I *had* hoped that Mr Tod, our new rector, would be saying as much at the whole-staff meeting first thing this morning. Unfortunately, he spent most of the morning reading through a list of regional circulars before reminding us to switch off the staffroom tea-urn when not in use.

Even more disappointingly, he did not take the opportunity to try and 'bond' the diverse elements of his new staff together. To explain, a degree of tension still exists between the former staffs of Parkland and Rockston, and it hasn't been helped by the appointments procedure for promoted posts in the new school, of which approximately 80% have gone to former Parkland teachers. Consequently, a split has already emerged, as was evidenced by the invisible boundary line displayed in staffroom seating arrangements at lunchtime: one half comprised Rockston staff, silently proclaiming ownership of 'their' staffroom by whispering quietly to each other and casting unpleasant glances the while across the room at our own coterie of Parkland teachers, all of us being made to feel distinctly unwelcome.

Nevertheless, time is a great healer, and I have every confidence that we shall soon all be pulling together in the best interests of Greenfield Academy – and its pupils, of course.

Tuesday – Second In-Service Day

A distressing request from Mr Tod to all guidance staff at this morning's staff meeting. In short, he is keen to transfer all available guidance data to a computer based record-keeping system, and has urged guidance staff to make the relevant records available to Mr Dick, his depute, by this afternoon.

Whilst happy to applaud the general thrust and nature of the scheme, I find myself unable to comply with the request due to the loss of my own year-group's records in the conflagration which wiped out Parkland High on the final day of last term. Although hardly to blame for this appalling arson attack, I was nevertheless at fault in not transferring the aforementioned records to Rockston – or Greenfield, rather – within the time-limits previously set out by Mr Tod. As yet, he is unaware of their loss – and I don't want to be around when he finds out.

Meanwhile, even more tension has arisen between members of staff, this time within the more immediate environs of the English department. At our first departmental meeting this afternoon Simon Young outlined his plans for the construction of a first-year syllabus and was about to go on to the second-year equivalent when he was halted in his tracks by the ill-spoken contributions of one Peter Chittick, a member of the department who has originated from the Rockston half of the staff. To be honest, I have seldom heard such illiterate and ungrammatical slovenliness, even from some of my former pupils!

'Naw, naw!' Chittick interjected uncouthly. 'Why're we no' havin' any meedja input fur the furst-year course? That kinda thing's a vital ingredient fur thae youngsters. See last year? Ah done a meedja unit wi' the furst year, an' they loved it – it's just the kinda thing thae kids need. So how about it?'

Momentarily taken aback, Simon promised to reconsider the inclusion of a media unit for the junior school, but I could see he was as startled by the style of the interruption as much as by the request itself.

And I must say I agree with him: in fact I was appalled, to be completely honest. The man's supposed to be teaching English, yet he can hardly speak it himself! To be frank, I am uneasy about forming a working relationship with him.

Wednesday

First day with our new pupils. Sadly, the tensions which exist between the staff of the two previous schools appear to be mirrored amongst the pupil population. For many of them, the prospect of a 'squerr-go outside' seems to hold more immediate likelihood of excitement than the academic pursuits on offer within the school building.

Needless to say, Tommy McShane and Alan McLeary are among the principal protagonists from the Parkland side, while a couple of extremely rough diamonds from Rockston – David Peck and Billy Cox – look increasingly likely to take our boys up on their death or glory challenge of a pitched battle after school.

As one of the guidance team responsible for this fourth-year group, the affair has already given me considerable cause for concern, even at this early stage in the term. I shared my worries with Pickup this afternoon, but he was too busy laughing at a memo from Richard Dick about a planned in-service course next month:

'Playground fights?' he glanced briefly at me. 'So what, Simpson? Let them knock lumps out of each other as far as I care. And if permanent injury results to any of the four of them, then so much the better!'

'But Mr Pickup –' I began.

'Oh, forget it,' he complained. 'You can't wetnurse them all the time, Simpson. Here,' he passed the depute's memo over to me. 'Take a look at this and cheer yourself up. Dick's wanting us all to go off on a jolly holiday together!'

And so it proved, in a manner of speaking. In an effort to encourage harmonious staff relationships, Mr Dick has arranged for a voluntary in-service session comprising two days in a distant hotel for the purposes of what he has termed a 'team-building exercise in situational leadership'. The option of attendance is open to all staff at assistant principal level and above and could therefore include Pickup and myself: personally, I was quite interested, but my colleague seemed to find the prospect hilarious in the extreme.

'You what?!' he laughed in my face. 'Two days listening to Dick Dick spouting forth about situational leadership – whatever the hell that's supposed to be when it's at home? The man couldn't situationally lead himself out of a chip shop, let alone tell us lot how to do it!'

I considered his comments rather unfair on Mr Dick, but held my counsel on the matter. I have often found this to be the best way to deal with Pickup.

Thursday

A memo in my pigeonhole this morning from Richard Dick. It wasn't alas, a personal invitation to join his course in situational leadership; rather, it was a peremptory reminder of my lateness in handing over the third-year guidance records. I gulped with concern upon reading it, but was pleased to notice that Peter Chittick appeared to be reading a similar reminder as well. Thinking to try and break some ice, I made further enquiry of him.

'Got a reminder from Mr Dick too, have you?'

'Aye,' he tossed his head with complete lack of concern. 'Silly wee tosser's gettin' all worked up about his guidance records.'

'Oh?' I queried, awash with innocence. 'Haven't you got round to handing *yours* in either, then?'

He shrugged a disaffected shoulder. 'Naw. Canny find them at the moment. Pretty sure ah seen them around the end o' June, but canny lay hands on them just now.' He paused in further contemplation of the note before him.

'Ah, stuff it!' he eventually declaimed before screwing up the memo into a tightly crunched ball and aiming it carefully at a wastepaper basket in the corner. 'Youse Parkland guys are full o' crap!'

So much for co-operation with the senior management team, I thought to myself. Personally, I inserted the memo into my daily diary and resolved to find a way of explaining my own situation to Dick as quickly as possible.

Friday

Another memo fron Dick Dick about my absent guidance records. As so often before, I took my worries to Mr Pickup at lunchtime. As so often before, he completely failed to appreciate my concerns, preferring instead to acquaint me with his latest thoughts about the situational leadership course, on which topic he has taken yet another of his amazing U-Turns.

'Never mind the guidance records, Morris,' he replied unceremoniously. 'Take a look at this.'

The sheet which he handed me seemed little more than a detailed account of Mr Dick's earlier memo on the subject, and I said so.

'Ah, but!' Pickup held a knowledgeable forefinger in the air: 'there are two important items of information on that sheet which make a world of difference, old son.'

'Oh?' I queried.

'Yes. Firstly, the type and dates of the course: this is a day-release job for selected applicants only, not part of the whole-school in-service programme.'

'So?'

'So it means an *extra* two days away from the bloody kids!' Pickup proclaimed excitedly.

'And secondly?' I queried.

'And secondly,' he exclaimed in triumph, 'Look at the travelling expenses details.'

I did as instructed, but could see little to explain the avaricious gleam which had arisen in Pickup's eyes. I raised my eyebrows in enquiry. 'Sorry,' I apologised. 'I'm not with you.'

'It's casual users' rate, for God's sake!' he practically exploded with excitement. 'And that's knocking on for a quid a mile these days. By the time we get down to the Hydro and back, we'll have clocked up a bloody fortune! Let's get our names down!'

I was about to question the educational validity of attending in-service provision on the basis of extra income to be generated through travelling expenses, but was cut short by the arrival of a worried first-year girl at the door, alerting staff to the fact that a major battle was about to take place in Ashvale Crescent between former pupils of Parkland High and former pupils of Rockston High.

A quick check from the staffroom window, out of which corner can be seen the end of Ashvale Crescent, revealed the truth of her report: approximately 30 pupils were lined up across the road, about to start a threatening march upon another 30 who were facing them. It looked likely to develop into an extremely ugly situation, so I began to hurry out of the staffroom to call a halt to the violence.

'Hang on a minute, Simpson!' called out Mr Pickup. 'Where the hell d'you think you're going?'

'To stop the fight!' I barked impatienty. 'Where d'you *think* I'm –'

'Get back in your seat!' he barked with equal impatience. 'That fight's taking place outwith school grounds, and as such it's got nothing to do with us!'

'You what?' I gasped with incredulity. 'You can't be serious. Those are our pupils, and –'

'Of course I'm serious!' he shouted. 'Now sit down!' To my astonishment, his claim seemed to be the first point of educational debate upon which the entire staffroom agreed. A chorus of murmured support arose, climaxed by Peter Chittick's assertion that 'the big guy' was 'spot-on', after which he picked up the telephone to call the police, pretending to be a resident of Ashvale Crescent who was worried about the incipient violence outside his front door.

Within ten minutes a panda car had arrived at the road-end and, within a further ten, two burly policemen had delivered a quartet of bruised and bleeding adolescents – McShane, McLeary, Peck and Cox, as if I couldn't have guessed – to the staffroom door.

Pickup it was who had the gall and sheer effrontery to thank the policemen for drawing to our attention this serious matter of indiscipline by pupils of Greenfield Academy, and further assuring them that the ringleaders would be dealt with severely.

How can the man sleep at nights, I wonder?

September

It is nearly always the case that, when two schools merge, there will be a degree of tension, even conflict, between the two groups of pupils who have been thrust together, so the fight which had occurred at the end of Greenfield Academy's first week in existence was not entirely unexpected, unwelcome though it might have been. And it certainly provided the *Parkland Gazette* with a good three pages of controversial copy.

The continued intractability of the two disparate *staff* groupings, however, was a source of some surprise to the new school's senior management team, and it was with this in mind that Richard Dick had planned his residential course as a means of breaking down the barriers, an event for which he had enlisted the particular support of Mr Boyd, the region's educational psychologist. Mr Dick thought highly of Jack Boyd, and he especially looked forward to a full programme of warm-up games and group-endeavour sessions which he knew Mr Boyd would be able to utilise in 'breaking-the-ice'. As Morris was to discover, there are a number of alternative, and more traditionally alcoholic, forms of 'ice-breakers' which can be equally effective at cementing friendships – even between such unlikely bed-fellows (so to speak) as himself and Peter Chittick.

Before the two days of September in-service, however, Morris discovered that his guidance role was going to be as problematic at Greenfield as it ever was at Parkland. And, as before, he was to discover that restive staff could give him as many problems as recalcitrant pupils.

Monday

Another awkward guidance problem reared its head this morning. Mr Potter, our principal teacher of technical (and one of the few ex-Rockston staff to be awarded a principal teacher's post), arrived at my office with a litany of voluble complaints about the behaviour of Michael Francis, one of his (and my guidance-sector) fourth year pupils.

'The boy's a disgrace, Mr Simpson!' he berated me, as if the child's behaviour was my own personal fault. 'He refuses to listen to instructions, and with a chisel in his hand he's a positive *danger* to other members of the class. And as well as that,' he continued angrily, 'the little toerag's continually breaking wind during my lessons – and I'm *certain* he's doing it to order! What are you going to *do* about it?'

Momentarily taken aback as to how I could discipline the alimentary functions of the boy, I was trying to frame a suitable reply when Potter thrust a document into my hand in further evidence of the child's ineducable qualities.

'There!' he spat in anger. 'Take a look at that!'

I must say I was appalled. The piece of paper, which I presumed to be an example of the boy's written classwork, was a disgraceful example of slovenly presentation – most of it completely illegible scrawlings. I nodded my head in solemn agreement with Mr Potter:

'I see what you mean, Brian,' I sympathised. 'If this is the kind of work that young Francis is presenting you with, then I'm going to have to see the boy –' and here I held up my forefinger to indicate the gravity of the situation '– and I might even think about calling in his parents as well.'

Potter looked puzzled for a moment, then shook his head in frustration.

'No, no, Simpson,' he pointed anew at the paper in my hands. 'That's not his work – that's my *conduct* report on the boy. It's putting down in writing all the punishments I've given him this term, plus the reasons behind them. It's for your *evidence* when you *suspend* him,' he concluded his explanation, clearly bewildered at my intitial incomprehension.

'Oh!' I gasped in sudden awareness. 'Sorry! I – um – sorry, but I thought this was – so this is your …?' I tailed off before peering disbelievingly at the hieroglyphic confusion before my eyes. 'So you'd like me to – uh …?'

'Suspend him!' Potter finished my sentence. 'Of course I would. That's what you're here for, isn't it?'

I endeavoured to explain the wider and remedial implications of a guidance teacher's job, but Potter wasn't having it.

'Oh, don't give me all that pastoral crap, Mr Simpson,' he cut in with impatience. 'The wee bugger's making my life a misery, and I want rid of him. Just suspend him for a few weeks, that's all I'm asking.'

'But on what precise *grounds*?' I queried, waving the indecipherable charge-sheet in front of me. 'What have I to tell his parents he's being suspended *for*?'

'Whatever you want,' Potter shrugged his shoulders. 'Try excessive farting, for all I care.' With which helpful suggestion he turned on his heel and went back to his woodwork.

So much for professionalism.

Tuesday

Another peremptory pigeon-hole reminder from Mr Dick about my missing guidance records this morning. He still neeeds these to complete the Greenfield Academy guidance database; I, for my part, have still been unable to pluck up courage to confess to the loss of said records during last session's end-of-term conflagration at Parkland High. At least I'm not the only one: Peter Chittick, my near-illiterate guidance colleague, appears to have lost his own records, though he seems a deal less concerned about the matter than I am.

As a temporary measure, I have resolved the issue by endeavouring to avoid Richard Dick at all costs. However, I am a little concerned about the feasibility of continuing such tactics during our two-day residential course on situational leadership which begins tomorrow. Dick Dick is in charge, and has promised a no-holds-barred session on management communication channels. I just hope guidance records don't come into it!

Wednesday

A slightly earlier rise than usual to collect Messrs Pickup, Chittick and Crumley, with whom I had offered to share transportation costs to our Hydro resort, the venue for Richard Dick's leadership course.

Sadly, they all seemed highly exited by the prospect of 'two days without a ruddy pupil in sight', as Pickup so artfully put it. Embarrassingly, Pickup further confirmed the tone for the journey by initiating a spirited chorus of 'Here We Go, Here We Go, Here We Go!' as my car set off from his house. I had hoped that the 40 minute trip would allow us to discuss some of the educational and management issues likely to arise during the next two days; alas, my passengers' conversations seemed exclusively concerned with mileage rates and the hoped-for provision of a swimming pool, jacuzzi and leisure facilities within our hotel.

To my further distress, much of the morning was taken up with what Dick Dick termed a 'role-play introductory session'. My early misgivings were confirmed by the highly embarrassing collection of 'psychological warm-ups and ice-breakers' to which we were subjected by Jack Boyd, one of the region's educational psychologists. Time does not permit an outline of the manifold revelations of personality which Mr Boyd encouraged us to make through a series of games which I thought more appropriate to a toddlers' playgroup than a gathering of consenting adults: suffice to say that the morning culminated with a thirty-strong circle of teachers hitting a balloon across the room at each other. As each of us threw the balloon at a colleague named by Boyd, we had to shout out the first word which came into our heads when thinking of that colleague. Sadly, I don't think Mr Pickup has yet forgiven me for my own contribution when asked to thrust the balloon in his direction ...

Mr Dick, of course, saw the game as an ideal means of breaking down barriers; for my own part, I worried immensely about the class-loads of children I had left behind, and in whose educational service I felt my time would have been more profitably spent than in a glorified play-session. Ultimately, I reckoned that our evening slot at the bar proved a more effective social lubricant, especially once Peter Chittick had raised the question of the missing guidance records.

He picked his moment carefully, I have to admit. It was just after Mr Dick had spent several minutes spouting forth about the more relaxed attitudes which could exist between management and staff during these socially-enlightened conference sessions:

'Oh yes,' he proffered a round of drinks to us all. 'This kind of session's often the best part of these courses – we can reveal secrets and share confidences that we probably wouldn't dare in the context of a more formal occasion, and all without the fear of any recrimination.'

He raised his eyebrows, clearly hoping for some no-holds-barred feedback on Greenfield Academy's management structure. In fact, the only comment in return was Peter Chittick's swift invention of a cock-and-bull story about his missing guidance records.

'Listen, Dick, ah've been meanin' tae tell you about thae records,' he explained uncouthly. 'Ah pit them in a box tae give ye, but ah think ma cleaner's chucked them out by mistake.'

Dick was speechless for a moment, and I sensed my own chance.

'Were – uh – the records which *I* passed on to you in that box as *well*, Peter?' I queried meaningfully, raising my eyebrows in frantic supplication. Luckily, he got my drift. Eventually.

'Eh?' he queried at first 'Whit d'ye – oh!' he suddenly caught on. 'Oh, aye. That's right. They wur!'

Mr Dick's jaw dropped as he considered the administrative nightmare which was about to confront him, but he could hardly say much in complaint, given the liberal nature of his earlier pronouncement. I don't think it had been the kind of revelation or confidence he'd had in mind, but it certainly cheered me up for the rest of the night.

So much so, that I expressed a willingness to join Pickup's 'after-hours' celebration in his room, where he, Crumley and Chittick had foregathered to consume several bottles of Guinness. Unfortunately, Pickup appears unacquainted with the demands of hotel etiquette, as evidenced by his request of the receptionist for a bottle-opener.

She had, he reported, looked severely over her glasses and informed him that 'Guests are not allowed to consume their own alcohol within hotel bedrooms. Sir.'

'It was that final "sir" that bugged me most of all,' Pickup complained upon return to the room. 'Snooty wee bitch,' he pronounced, before making do with the edge of a clenched fist and the corner of a dressing table instead. The first bottle creamed gloriously over the lip, and we settled down for our nightcap.

'Good initiative, Pickup,' I ventured a minor joke: 'Otherwise it might have been collapse of stout party. Eh?'

Pickup curled an uncomprehending lip. 'What? What are you on about *now*, Simpson?' he demanded, swinging a bottle to his lips.

'Never mind,' I sighed. I think he'd had too much to drink. Some several hours (and sixteen bottles) later, I think the same could have been said of the rest of us. The only event I can remember with any clarity is my offering to kiss Peter Chittick goodnight in gratitude for his assistance over the missing guidance records.

Fortunately, he refused.

Thursday

Unfortunately, Mr Pickup and I slept in this morning. Thus it was that we were unable to witness the edifying sight of Richard Dick at the breakfast table, clad in tracksuit top and shorts after his morning run, and tucking in to a breakfast of fresh yoghurt, muesli and fruit juice.

'You're lucky you missed it,' muttered George Crumley as we staggered in to the conference room with minutes to spare. 'I got a lecture on calorific values and cholestorol levels in my bacon and egg that'd make your hair turn grey. Healthy little git,' he swore as Mr Dick took up position at the front of the room and began an explanation of situational leadership styles.

'At last,' I whispered blearily to Pickup. 'This is what we're supposed to be here for.' Alas, my hopes were frustrated by yet another interminable selection of role-plays about fictitious events in the world of business, and about how we would react to these in terms of our likely management and leadership decisions. The accompanying tick-charts which Dick had provided asked for an honest self-evaluation of our likely management styles – were we 'autocratic, or consensual?' it queried of us. Furthermore, Dick explained, for each task we were to evaluate what he called our 'confidence levels' and our 'competence levels'.

'For each task, you'll find these will vary,' he explained brightly. 'In some tasks, you'll have a very high competence level, but a very low confidence level. For others, it might be high confidence, low competence. And sometimes you'll have highs in both confidence *and* competence!'

The only combination he singularly *failed* to mention was that which he ultimately accorded to me in his assessment of my own contributions some two hours later.

'Hmm,' he mused in dismay as he surveyed my decision-making chart. 'Sorry, Morris: you seem to have scored "fours" across the board. Low confidence throughout,' he explained. 'And even lower competence,' he added in disappointment. 'Never mind,' he tossed his head brightly again, '– why don't you look on it as a starting-point for improvement?' With which comforting advice he moved on to Mr Pickup.

My colleague's attempts at circling decision points, I happened to know, had been made at complete random – the man had spent the entire morning crouched over his pocket calculator, totting up the mileage payments he was likely to accrue as a result of our trip down the coast – so it was particularly galling to hear Richard Dick congratulate him on 'some very perceptive decisions, Mr Pickup'. I nearly choked on my digestive biscuit at morning coffee as Pickup crowed about the leadership potential he claimed to have displayed during the session.

'Hmmph,' I muttered in bad grace. 'From what I could see, you had a random success rate which was equivalent to a monkey's, Pickup!'

'Yes,' he nodded smoothly – 'and it was still twice as high as your own, Simpson. Not to mention the fact that I reckon a monkey would make a damned sight better job of running the education system than most of the jokers who are doing it at present!'

The rest of the day followed a broadly similar pattern, which saw my confidence and competence levels constantly denigrated, until I found myself completely demoralised and wishing I had never volunteered for the course. The brightest spot of the day was our departure from the hotel and the prospect of getting back to teaching tomorrow.

As Pickup got out of the car at 4 o'clock, he leaned over, checked the mileage reading carefully and handed me some petrol money.

'There you are, Morris,' he smiled broadly. 'Get our claims in tomorrow, and we should all be rolling in it come next pay-day!'

I shook my head sorrowfully and bade him farewell. What a mercenary attitude to education!

Friday

It's all very well going off on these in-service courses, but the mountain of correction which awaited me when I got into school today made me wonder if it was really worth it. Ten class-loads of essay and comprehension assessments, combined with the unholy mess which each cover-teacher had left behind, made me quail with despair when I walked back into my classroom.

As if that wasn't enough to be going on with, my free period today – last one this afternoon – saw me wading through a host of guidance-related issues which had built up in my absence. Mr Potter's further complaints about Michael Francis comprised the bulk of the material, and my heart sank to witness him frogmarching the boy towards my office at 3.55 this afternoon.

'He's done it again, Mr Simpson' Potter barked, a handkerchief pressed against his nose. 'What are you going to *do* about it?'

I was about to embark upon a pastoral – if not medical – discussion with pupil and master when the bell rang. Potter was transformed instantaneously.

'Oh!' his ear cocked and his face lightened. 'That's the bell!' he remarked needlessly. 'I'll have to go, Simpson. Leave it till next week, eh?' With which he turned tail and left the room.

I looked askance at Michael Francis and dismissed him forthwith. Potter, Pickup told me later, hit the playground running.

Once again, so much for professionalism.

October

Time used to be when a pupil who misbehaved in class would be dealt with by the teacher of that class. Not any more.

As we have already discovered, a rigid hierarchical structure now exists in most schools, whereby a disobedient child will be passed from one level of authority to the next, depending upon the seriousness of the offence and the level of expected retribution. In fact, it can often take so long for this to happen that by the time any punishment is issued, the miscreant has usually forgotten what he or she has done to deserve it in the first place, but this is of little consequence. Whatever offence has taken place will have been duly recorded, usually in triplicate, and the accumulated paperwork thereof will have been appropriately filed and stored.

For the average class teacher, the first stage in such a referral procedure is to send any errant pupil to the principal teacher of his or her department. On the occasion of a principal teacher experiencing disciplinary unrest, of course, the next stage in the line-management structure would be to refer the matter to the appropriate guidance teacher, hence Mr Potter's frequent sallies along the corridor to Morris's office.

In Greenfield Academy, however, as in many other schools, a new disciplinary line-structure was going to have to be drawn up which took cognizance of the fact that, in many departments, the ordinary class teacher would be unable to refer problems to a principal teacher owing to the gradual erosion of such posts on the (ostensible) grounds of pupil numbers within a school, as well as on the (actual) grounds of financial restraint. By such sophistry were education departments, and schools, able to place teachers in positions of responsibility for running departments without having to pay them for doing so. Of course, you could hardly call such people principal teachers if you weren't going to pay them a principal teacher's salary. And it was difficult to call a meeting for principal teachers when half of those attending would therefore only be assistant principal teachers. But Mr Tod had already thought of that one, as the Simpson diaries for October will explain.

Monday

Mr Tod has given a new name to the weekly meeting of principal teachers: henceforth it is to be known as the meeting of departmental leaders. The alteration is due to the increasing percentage of staff who have been accorded the privilege of running a department but without the concomitant title – and salary – of a principal teacher.

Mr Pickup – assistant principal teacher of religious education – is a case in point, and he emerged from this morning's gathering with an even more ferocious scowl than usual. It was due, I soon discovered, to a decision which had been taken at this morning's meeting.

'Bloody Dick!' he ungraciously termed our depute head teacher. 'Tod's put him in charge of the school development plan

– as if the little squirt didn't have enough to bother us about already.'

I raised an enquiring eyebrow. 'Oh? And what's so awful about that?'

'It means we're supposed to *produce* something now! When Tod was looking after it, nobody needed to bother. Now that Dick's been handed another ruddy remit he'll be like a terrier with a rat between its teeth. God help us!' he smote his brow. 'We're all supposed to produce a departmental development plan between now and a week on Friday.'

'Oh?' I enquired again. 'And what does that entail?'

'Two hundredweight of bumf, Simpson, that's what it entails!' Pickup replied rudely. 'Endless reams of my aims and objectives from now until next Easter – where do I see the department going, how am I going to achieve my objectives, all that sort of crap – and it's not as if any bugger's going to actually *read* the ruddy thing in the first place!'

'No?' I questioned him yet again.

'No, of course not!' he shook his head. 'As long as Dick Dick's got fourteen departmental returns in his sweaty little paws, then he can wave them about and say he's got a whole-school development plan in operation. But don't expect him to actually *look* at the things!'

I thought Mr Pickup was displaying an appalling lack of trust in Richard Dick's professionalism, and said as much at once.

'Balls!' swore Pickup in yet another unconscionable display of boorishness. 'I could fill the ruddy report with nursery rhymes if I wanted, and he'd never be any the wiser.'

I gave up. 'You're incorrigible, Pickup!' I slapped him on the back. 'I don't know why I still bother listening to you.'

'Hmmph,' he growled. 'Because I'm the only one in this place that talks any sense – and you know it!' he declaimed authoritatively.

I smiled in patient consolation. He really is the limit.

Tuesday

Today saw the arrival of Matthew Gordon, a new member of the geography department. He wandered tentatively into the staffroom at ten to nine – and then wandered tentatively back out again.

'Ah,' nodded Miss Peters, acting principal teacher of modern languages during the illness of Mrs Leleu. 'So *that's* Mr Gordon ...'

'And who's he?' I queried.

'New member of the geography department – sort of,' she explained.

'How d'you mean, sort of?'

'Mr Tod warned us about him at yesterday's departmental leaders' meeting,' she explained. 'He's a bit of a school phobic, apparently. Been in four different schools since he started – always moved on.'

'But why? Didn't he like any of them?'

'Don't know. Never in any of them long enough to find out, I gather. Can't be put in charge of any classes because he's so incompetent, plus he's got a sick-record that would make a terminal cancer patient look positively healthy.'

'So why's he been sent *here*, then?' I asked, completely incredulous that such a situation could exist within today's education system.

'Usual merry-go-round,' Miss Peters shrugged her shoulders. 'The divisional education officer passes him from school to school to lighten the load on everybody.'

'Plus,' cut in Mr Pickup from across the coffee table, 'the DEO reckons we've got a good record for accommodating incompetents and misfits in this place already.'

I studiously ignored his meaningful stare in my direction, and suggested to Miss Peters that the authority would be better off sacking him if he was so completely useless. She looked puzzled.

'Sack him?' she raised an upper lip in question. 'How can they? It's very difficult to *prove* anything, Morris. Very difficult indeed.'

I shook my head in disbelief. To my mind, her previous testimony had been proof enough of the man's unsuitability to remain in employment, but she seemed to be of the opinion that the authority would have difficulty in 'making anything stick', and had therefore decided to adopt a *laissez-faire* approach. No wonder our schools are in such a state.

Wednesday

A very busy day: much of this morning was taken up with Mr Potter's continued insistence that I suspend Michael Francis for his perpetual breaking of wind in Potter's technical classroom. I had thought my request to Mr Potter that he provide written evidence of all such instances of classroom disruption would be enough to calm the storm for a while – being a technical teacher, Potter doesn't really like having to write *anything* down – but, alas, he has now presented me with a detailed and elaborate (if barely legible) listing of every occasion when Michael Francis claims to have lost control of his sphincter muscle.

I find it hard to believe that a grown man should seem so worked up about such a pathetic affair – to my mind Potter's actions have blown the matter up, so to speak, out of all proportion. He has demanded punitive action on Fraser by the end of the week, but I can't imagine how to phrase any suspension note to the boy's parents.

Meanwhile, my guidance responsibilities have made me fall further behind in classroom preparation: the first-years are supposed to be doing a Hallowe'en presentation on Friday, plus my fourth-year class (Michael Francis included) are supposed to be starting a theme-study dealing with family relationships on the same day. Where can I find the time for it all?

Thursday

Mr Pickup – who still seems excessively dismayed about the need to provide a development plan by a week tomorrow – was in temporarily bright humour this morning upon receipt of his salary slip, which included details of his successful claim for travelling expenses against last month's trip to our in-service course on situational leadership.

'Great!' he ripped the perforated edging from the envelope, smacking his lips in anticipation. 'Travelling eccies at last: this should see us all right for a small libation tomorrow evening, eh Morris?'

'Mmm,' I smiled wearily as I examined my own pay-slip, still thinking of Halowe'en poems and family trees. 'A couple of pints, anyway,' I concurred.

'Hmph,' snorted Pickup, '– I think we'll do better than that! Chittick and Crumley are pooling their take as well,' he explained, in reference to our travelling companions on the days in question, 'so we should have quite a kitty.'

'That'll be a help, certainly,' I admitted, 'but I can't see – hang on!' I pulled myself up as I squinted over Pickup's elbow at the figure against his travelling expenses code. '*How* much is that you've claimed for?' I queried with incredulity.

Pickup looked surprised. 'Same as you, I presume,' he gently prised my salary slip from my hand before looking at me with equal incredulity.

'What the hell's this, Morris?' he burst out. 'You've only claimed a *quarter* of what I've claimed.'

'Well, of course I have!' I countered. 'There were four of us in the car and we split the petrol. So I only claimed quarter-rate on the mileage. That's fair enough, isn't it?'

'Morris!' Pickup smote his brow for the second time this week. '*I* know there were four of us in the car. *You* know there were four of us in the car. Chittick and *Crumley* know there were four of us in the car. But the regional *offices* don't know there were four of us in the car! We *all* claim mileage allowance for our *own* cars, don't you realise that? It's the only bloody perk of the job we've got!'

I was dumbfounded, I have to admit. 'And Chittick and Crumley?' I queried tentatively. Will they have –'

'Oh, for God's sake don't be so wet, Morris,' he exclaimed angrily. 'Of *course* they will have – haven't you learned *anything* in nearly eight years of teaching?'

At first, I wondered if Pickup's anger was due to the possibility of their being found out in defrauding the education authority because of my own claim; however, he assured me that this was unlikely as no such checks had ever been made before, on the grounds that teachers would be grossly offended should their integrity be called into question in this fashion. The real reason behind his anger, it transpired, was the sudden reduction of tomorrow night's beer kitty which my ethical stand had occasioned.

I promised to make it up from my own pocket instead.

Friday

A traumatic day.

To begin with, my first-year Hallowe'en project had to be abandoned on the grounds of a complaint from Andrew Carswell's father. Having already crossed swords with our ex-school board chairman over the matter of the English department's reading list some two years ago now, I decided that discretion would be the better part of valour on this occasion. Although unwilling to concede that our class display of witches' broomsticks could be considered an 'incitement to Satanism and the black arts', as Mr Carswell claimed, I had little energy to put up a fight and decided to let the matter rest. I put the materials away and we watched a video instead.

In any case, I was already exhausted over the business of my fourth-year project on family trees – also abandoned, alas. Unfortunately, I had been unaware of the regional prohibition on such projects owing to the likely problems which can arise in these days of unstable and short-term family relationships. Suffice to say that when Rothesay Kyle started to produce a family tree it began to resemble a lineage more akin to the protagonists of *War and Peace* than a straightforward delineation of her parents, grandparents and blood relations.

The poor girl, I soon began to recall, has had five different stepfathers in the course of her young life (the position was complicated somewhat by her insistence upon calling the first four of these men her 'uncles', so that differentiation from her mother's seven brothers proved harder to illustrate). And when we tried to trace the subsequent progeny of her natural father – a fecund individual, if all accounts are to be believed – then matters became *really* complicated.

It was all a source of much hilarity for the ululant Michael Francis, who lost little opportunity to goad the poor girl about her background, and it wasn't long before I realised the grounds of our education authority's advice in avoiding such topics. The only consolatory factor to arise from the period was the opportunity to suspend young Fraser for the gross profanity which he used to describe Rothesay's lack of conventional parentage.

As I explained to Pickup in the Rockston Arms that evening, swearing in the presence of a teacher was likely to be more acceptable as a reason for suspension than Mr Potter's unending complaints about the boy's alimentary malfunctions – but at least the suspension has shut Potter up, for the moment at least.

Otherwise, our conversation for the evening centred on two topics: Mr Pickup's development plan and the absence from school today of Matthew Gordon, who had apparently telephoned news of his absence this morning on the grounds of a 'viral infection'. Enough said.

On the topic of the school development plan, Pickup's depression seemed to have mysteriously lifted so that when George Crumley brought up his own such concerns, Pickup looked positively smug.

'Not got it done yet, George?' he questioned innocently. 'Just put the finishing touches to mine this morning, if you're interested?'

'What?' George Crumley nearly choked on his lager. 'You can't have! Mine's only down to the bottom of the first page.'

'Tsk, tsk,' Pickup shook his head. 'It's all a question of prioritising matters – as I said to Mr Dick when I handed over my development plan this afternoon.'

Our disbelief knew no bounds, so after Pickup had purchased another round from the seemingly bottomless pit of money which had formed the evening's subsidised drinking session, he consented to let us in on the details.

Having sworn us all to absolute secrecy, he confessed that his initially jocular remarks to me on Monday about filling in his report with nursery rhymes had given him further pause for subsequent thought. Having spent the best part of Monday evening concocting a jargon-laden introductory section of 'short-term and long-term objective priorities for religious education in Greenfield Academy', he had adjudged the work to be of such monumental tedium that anyone reading further than its first two pages would be liable to catatonic indifference.

'So,' he announced carelessly, 'I filled up the rest of it with a reprint of the school rules and a copy of the regional policies on sexism and racism. Made for a pretty fat document,' he added needlessly, 'and it certainly impressed Tricky Dicky.'

We were agog with admiration – and concern.

'But surely he'll find out?' I queried. 'What'll you do *then*?'

'No chance, Simpson,' explained Pickup confidently. 'Like I said – nobody ever reads these things. Just so long as they're *there*, that's all that matters.'

It seems a high-risk strategy to me. Time, no doubt, will tell.

November

To an outsider, it is a source of some amazement to discover the veritable profusion of documentation which is required to run a school in this paper-strewn age. Every decision, every action, every policy document and every management structure process has to be accompanied by several hundred sheets of paper which are intended to perform at least four separate functions.

Take the example of a school policy on discipline, for example: firstly, there must be a piece of paper which tells what the policy is; secondly, there must be a piece of paper which outlines how the policy will be implemented; thirdly, there must be a piece of paper which records how the policy has *been* implemented; and finally there must be a piece of paper which records how successful – or unsuccessful – the policy has been. In some schools, of course, the fourth sheet of paper can spawn yet *another* sheaf of documents in the guise of an 'ongoing evaluation policy'.

It is an entire industry. The introduction of word-processors and desk top publishing systems to the electronic armoury of most schools would appear to make the task of paper management much simpler and more manageable. Of course it does no such thing; quite the reverse, in fact.

The availability of desk top publishing systems simply encourages teachers like Richard Dick to produce more, and even more, reams of paper in a ceaseless attempt to reassure colleagues and superiors of their educational worth. Even Mr Pickup, as we have just seen, thought he had found a way to work the system to his professional advantage, only with even less expenditure of effort than Mr Dick. Time would tell whether his deception over the development plan would be discovered. For the moment, he felt confident it would not.

Mr Dick's increasing involvement with the development plan, and other matters of a managerial bent, was only to be expected. Apart from Dick's ready willingness to embrace any task which kept him away from children, it had also become noticeable within Greenfield Academy that Mr Tod seemed to be following the managerial style of John Ross, his recently retired predecessor, by retreating within the confines of his study as often as decency would allow. It was a process which was to continue as the months went by, until Tod felt himself as fully insulated as possible from the everyday concerns of school life.

Had his finger been more closely on the pulse of school activities, Mr Tod might have been more aware of the unrest which was brewing within the ranks of his school cleaners over the recent alteration in their terms of employment. For Morris, the regional decision to utilise the services of a private contractor had been one of which he fully approved. The savings which would therby accrue were a source of financial satisfaction to the region, of course, and Morris had every confidence that such savings would be ploughed back into improved educational provision.

Not everyone would agree with such an interpretation, of course, but Morris felt the arrangements were to be commended, as his November diary will explain.

Monday

This has been the first day of our new cleaning arrangements provided by Kleenup, the regionally-appointed private company charged with the task of keeping Greenfield Academy spotless – and at a third of the previous cost of the old authority-sponsored contract, I might add.

Apart from a slightly smaller workforce, there doesn't actually seem to be that much difference under the new regime: Mrs Auld, my regular cleaner, would still appear to be in charge of my room, and she certainly looked a good deal smarter when she turned up for duty this afternoon, clad in shining corporate overalls and waistcoat, her (ex-regional) brushes and mops alike adorned with the Kleenup company logo. I must say it all looked very professional, and I congratulated her on her appearance as I prepared to leave for home.

'Hmmph!' she scoffed contemptuously. 'Privatised crap!'

I didn't wish to get into a political argument with the woman, but she persisted in a laborious explanation concerning the changes to her conditions of service and loss of pension rights which have unfortunately transpired since her new employers won the regional cleaning contract. My own view is that she certainly wasn't *forced* into accepting the job with Kleenup, but I decided to keep my own counsel with a vague expression of personal sympathy whilst reminding her that regional economy and efficiency were more urgently required under today's economic climate than might have hitherto been the case.

'Hah!' she scoffed once more, wielding a stiff-bristled sweeping brush with a ferocity I'd seldom witnessed before. 'Economy "n" efficiency's fine, Mr Simpson. But slave labour's supposed tae've went oot the door hundreds o' years ago, intit?'

I nodded in tacit agreement and decided to quietly edge from her presence, but not before she flailed a mop aggressively in my direction.

'How the hell ah'm supposed tae clean the same number o' rooms as *four* folk cleaned *last* week, ah dunno. Kin *you* tell me? Kin ye?'

'No. No, I'm afraid I can't, Mrs Auld,' I nodded sympathetically before sidling out of the classroom as surreptitiously as tact

would allow. Despite her protestations to the contrary, I can't help feeling that Mrs Auld's workrate is bound to be improved by the more stringent labour control exercised by her new employers. And who knows? My room might even be cleaner as well.

Tuesday

Mr Tod seems to have taken to communication by memorandum only. He insists upon remaining within the confines of his rectorial study for the duration of most academic days, with the sole exception of Rotary luncheon occasions.

Thus, our ambitious depute Mr Dick finds himself the harbinger of constant and peremptory requests of an administrative nature which might otherwise have emanated from our noble head. Not that Mr Dick seems to mind; in fact, he appears to positively relish the position.

'And one final item,' he concluded a hastily-convened staff meeting at lunch-time today. 'Mr Tod's becoming very anxious about the number of departmental development plans which he's yet to receive. Could I remind all of you,' he glanced sharply in the direction of Messrs Crumley, Henderson and Dunbar, 'that these development plans were due in last week. Why can't you take a leaf out of Mr Pickup's book? Eh? Three weeks early, and a finely balanced piece of forward planning for an integrationist whole-school policy in religious education.'

It was too much for Mr Crumley, who practically choked into his coffee mug. Like myself, he was only too well aware that Pickup's massive tome of educational miasma consisted of two introductory pages on the aforementioned development plan, followed by another 36 carefully transferred sheets of A4 consisting of the school rules plus a straight copy of the regional policies on sexism and racism. Confident that such documents need only *exist* and need never actually be *consulted* by anyone, Pickup had decided to save himself the enormous effort involved in producing one and – at Dick's congratulatory remarks – lounged back in his chair, a beatific grin across his face at such public proof of the hypothesis.

I still think it's a high-risk strategy, and told him as much after Dick Dick had left the staffroom.

'Nonsense, Simpson!' he chortled. 'That document'll never be out of Dick's drawer between now and kingdom come.' I shook my head in doubt, but Pickup continued forcefully: 'Look, you've just heard Dick proclaiming it the best piece of educational research since Piaget's bloody cognitive development theory, and making a complete arse of himself in the process to those of us who know what's really in it. The only chance of him ever being any the wiser's if he has to produce it for any of the divisional officers who pay us a call to make sure we're generating enough paperwork! And I don't think *that's* very likely,' he mused ruefully. 'We haven't seen any of *them* since the day we opened!'

I shook my head mournfully and decided to go and tidy out my room instead. Mrs Auld didn't seem to have made a very thorough job of it last night.

Wednesday

We are still experiencing staffing problems, exacerbated by the apparent unwillingness of certain staff to overcome minor ailments in attempting to get into the work for which the regional council pays them!

In particular, I am incensed by the continued absence of Matthew Gordon, whose newest sick-line arrived with the school office this morning. His viral complaint has now, alas, turned into a series of dizzy spells which continue to make him unavailable for work. George Crumley, his principal teacher, shook his head in amazement at the latest display of imaginative diagnosis displayed by Mr Gordon's health centre.

'God knows how he can fool them!' he swore in exasperation. 'Because he certainly doesn't fool me! And as if I didn't have enough on my plate with a departmental development plan to finish: now I'll have to get a whole new set of lessons ready for the PE supply teacher they've sent!'

I shook my head in sympathy. 'Why don't the education authorities do something about him?' I queried. 'He does seem to be a bit of a liability, after all. And his illnesses seem pretty suspect to me ...'

'Suspect?' laughed Crumley. 'They're pure bloody fiction, Simpson. But,' – and here he raised a warning finger in the air – 'just try proving anything. He'd have the union down on us like a ton of bricks for harrassing sick employees.'

I hardly think that a responsible trade union such as ours would behave in such a fashion, but it seems unlikely they'd have the chance: after all, the authorities don't seem to be doing much about it in the first place!

It's all very difficult to stomach, especially for teachers of real dedication. Like myself.

Thursday

I wonder if Matthew Gordon would be the sort of chap willing to empty his own classroom bin, as I had to do this morning, due to the continued absence of any apparent cleansing activities in Room C17. I doubt it very much. I'm going to have some stern words with Mrs Auld the next time I see her.

Later on in the day, I thought we were at least going to have some regional action over the case of Matthew Gordon's repeated absences, because at half past three our divisional education officer's car drew up in the school playground. Hastily, I scurried along to tell Mr Crumley that Dangerous Dan Baxter was in town, so that he could marshal his evidence in plenty of time. However, I was surprised to meet Mr Baxter and my *own* principal teacher, Simon Young, in earnest conversation as I entered the staffroom. In fact, Baxter was visiting the school on a spot of pre-appraisal information gathering about one of his senior advisers – or so I eventually discovered after a lengthy dressing-down from Simon Young after Baxter's departure!

To explain, Mr Baxter broke off his conversation with Simon when I entered the room and fixed me with a smile of patent insincerity:

'Ah, Mr Simpson,' he oozed quietly. 'Perhaps you could help us out here?'

'Certainly, Mr Baxter,' I smiled nervously. 'If I can, that is.'

'Nothing important, really,' he lied. 'Just wondered how you'd been getting on with Kenny Cameron, that's all.'

'Kenny who?' I queried.

'Cameron. Kenny Cameron. Chief languages adviser, with special responsibilty for English.'

'Sorry?' I queried again, only becoming aware of Simon Young's frantic hand signals after it was all too late. 'Never heard of him, I'm afraid.'

Baxter drew a photograph from his breast pocket.

'Doesn't look at all familiar, then?'

'Um,' I floundered uncertainly, glancing quickly at Simon's anguished features. 'Well, maybe – uh – maybe that's – uh – him? Is it?' I tailed off in confusion.

'Thank-you, Mr Simpson,' Baxter clenched his jaws firmly shut and replaced the photograph in his pocket. 'You've told me all I need to know.' With which concluding statement he turned on his heel and marched sternly out of the staffroom.

'You bloody great cretin, Morris!' swore Simon – quite unreasonably, I thought – 'He was in here checking up on Kenny Cameron's activities in schools before his appraisal interview next week, and I'd just finished telling him how Kenny was never out of the place, what with helping us in our language development plans, departmental development plans, and whole-school development plans! Kenny?' says I. 'A great guy, Mr Baxter. Always there when we need him!'

'But I've never seen him!' I protested. 'And –'

'Yes you have!' Simon corrected me. 'He was at our Christmas party last year, and –'

'Well, I don't remember him, and anyway, coming to a Christmas party hardly constitutes giving constructive curricular guidance, does it?'

'Doesn't matter, Morris,' argued Simon angrily. 'Kenny Cameron's a good mate of mine since university days, and I'm not wanting Dan Baxter of all people to have any grounds for nailing him. Unfortunately,' he shook his head scornfully, 'you've just given him the perfect ammunition for a hatchet-job!'

Honestly! I didn't know which to be more angry about: the fact that I was being pilloried for not recognising a complete and utter stranger, or the fact that Dan Baxter was spending valuable time trying to find fault with one of his colleagues, when I understood that appraisal was supposed to be about the accentuation and encouragement of positive career elements! Not to mention the fact that – in my opinion – he'd be better off tracking down the *real* layabouts – like Matthew Gordon, for example!

Friday

I have decided to lodge a formal complaint about the state of my room. I don't think Mrs Auld's been near it all week except to pile small heaps of rubbish into larger accumulations in each corner of the room. The final straw was finding some day-old bubble-gum on the underside of a desk which I was moving this morning preparatory to some improvised drama with the first year. It was still soggy, so took several minutes to clean off my fingernails, and was an obvious indication of our private cleaning contractor's appalling standards of quality control.

I tried to pass on my displeasure to Mrs Auld at 4 o'clock, but the woman would not even stay to hear me out. A bedraggled and sweat-stained figure simply advised me:

'Ah've no time fur a chat, Mr Simpson. Three rooms tae polish before hauf-four. Ah'll be round tae yours in, eh,' – she thought briefly – 'eh, around two weeks. See you.'

I was dumbfounded. Though not as much, I have to say, as Mr Pickup was when he discovered that Mr Cameron, regional adviser, was in school this morning to pick up our development plans!

First of all, however, the man was apparently at pains to make my acquaintance:

'Good morning,' he greeted me sourly at morning interval, his ill-temper obvious to see. 'You're Morris Simpson, aren't you?'

I nodded assent, upon which he pointed both forefingers at his own face and set his mouth in firm displeasure.

'Me Kenny Cameron. Me senior adviser. Remember it, Judas. OK?'

With which peremptory introduction he decanted to Richard Dick's office for the removal – and study – of all departmental development plans, as so obviously instructed by Dan Baxter. Pickup was devastated.

'Bloody hell!' he swore aggressively. 'The bastard's actually taking them away to read them!'

'Ah-hah, Mr Pickup,' I spoke in sad triumph. 'Be sure your sins will find you out, eh?'

For a moment, he seemed quite forlorn. And then, suddenly, his face lightened.

'D'you think so, Morris? I'm not so sure actually. He's taking them away, certainly. But I wonder,' he pondered thoughtfully, 'I really wonder – d'you think he'll ever actually *read* them?'

'But of course he will!' I expostulated. 'He's a senior adviser, for heaven's sake!'

Pickup just laughed. 'Exactly, Simpson! That's exactly my point! I rest my case.'

I find it difficult to share his confidence.

December

Rockston Health Centre

Certificate of illness

Name: Matthew Gordon
Nature of illness: viral complaint
Period of certifiable sick-leave: four weeks

Signed:..
....

Mr Pickup's sanguine approach to the removal of his school development plan for further study by the advisorate had much to commend it. Why should he worry about something over which he had no further control? Even more sanguine, of course, was Matthew Gordon, whose lengthy illness and protracted absence caused little genuine surprise to anyone except Morris, for whom such an ill-concealed lack of professionalism was nothing short of a disgrace.

On the question of professionalism, Mr Tod had been using his newly-discovered study time to good effect. Shielded from the rigours and practical demands of running a school, he was happy to leave it all up to Richard Dick whilst he got on with the long-delayed task of catching up on his management-skills reading. In particular, he was keen to develop a mission statement for the school in readiness for the new school prospectus, and as a first step in that direction he took the rare step of issuing a communication to all members of staff. Standards, he felt, needed to be improved.

Monday

Mr Tod's on a professionalism drive. He's been stung into activity by the national publication of last session's examination results. Although, as a newly-merged school, Greenfield Academy was saved from any exposure of its academic record by virtue of our non-existence at the time of compilation, it couldn't have failed to escape the attention of our more perceptive parents that both Parkland High and Rockston High – the two Greenfield progenitors – *also* failed to make an appearance on the listing. As with last year's list, schools with an academic pass rate of less than 5% continue to be deemed unworthy of inclusion.

As a consequence of this, and of his recently attended management training course, our esteemed headteacher has seen fit to set certain performance indicators and standards to be achieved by all departments. Henceforth, he is anxious to initiate a monitoring programme of our examination predictions, with an ultimate aim of – and I quote – 'a 23% upturn in performance over the next academic year.'

Personally, I have a firmly-held belief that education is about so much *more* than examination results; nevertheless, there were some other aspects of Mr Tod's staff memorandum this morning in which I felt that he had a valid point or two. In particular, I couldn't help but notice his desire for 'high standards of staff dress and behaviour, aspects of school ethos which contribute so much to the parents' perceptions of Greenfield Academy as a caring institute of professional integrity.'

'Loada crap!' cursed the unseemly Peter Chittick (English department) as he thrust the memo forcefully into a nearby wastepaper basket.

I disagreeed strongly, and reminded Chittick that our 'outward and visible signs were an indication of our inward and spiritual professionalism' – but he just gawped uncomprehendingly at me.

'Well, look at it this way, Peter,' I explained, passing by on the reference for ease of discussion, '– don't you think it creates a terrible impression to have parents or visitors to the school meeting staff from the PE department who haven't seen a tie since the day they graduated? And even – if you don't mind me saying so –' I frowned in his own direction, '– English teachers who think a leather jacket and a pair of stonewashed jeans are the height of sartorial elegance?'

I thought for a moment he was going to hit me, but he calmed himself enough to make the very forcible point – with both hands on my lapels, mark you – that as far as he was concerned the staff at Greenfield Academy – especially Peter Chittick – were about the most professional group of people he had ever come across, no matter their appearance.

'But, Peter!' I started once again, before noticing, out of the corner of my eye, Messrs Pickup and Dunbar – two of our most ardent professionals – having a paper aeroplane race with their respective copies of Mr Tod's memorandum.

I decided to let the matter rest.

Tuesday

Further evidence arose this morning of the less-than-professional approach of certain staff who seem more intent on their own personal interests than the greater good of the school.

Fiona Pratt – only recently returned from eight months of maternity leave – reported absent today on what she termed 'sympathetic leave' for her cholic-affected infant. I wouldn't mind so much, except that her pony-tailed spouse (one of our latter-day supply teachers back at Parkland High) is supposed to have taken on the role of house-husband in their modern-day relationship, so goodness knows why *he* can't nurse the wretched child!

Needless to say, Matthew Gordon of the geography department has still not made an appearance during his eight weeks of tenure: the current sick-line (for his viral complaint) was supposed to run out this week, but I dare say he'll be sending in another before long.

Meanwhile, I'm sorry to report that Mrs Auld – my recently-privatised cleaner – seems a broken woman. Having prepared a stern letter of complaint to Kleenup, her employers, over the continued Augean nature of my classroom, I find myself unwilling to send it after viewing the poor woman's exhaustion when I raised the matter this afternoon.

'Aye, fine, Mr Simpson,' was all she could mutter sadly as I started my complaint about the filthy condition of the classroom. Shaking her head slowly, she muttered something about the 24 rooms for whose cleanlines she was now responsible during her 55-minute shift, before promising, 'Ah'll see whit ah kin do. As soon as ah kin find some dusters'n'some polish. OK?' she sighed, before dragging herself downstairs in search of adequate cleansing materials.

Honestly. Between absentee teachers and unhygienic classrooms, Mr Tod's obviously got a real battle on his hands in any drive for an improvement in professional standards in this place!

Wednesday

I can't believe it. Guess who arrived as temporary supply cover for Fiona Pratt this morning? Martin Pratt, no less!

Imagine! He turns up for a spell of overpaid child-minding with a telephone-number salary for his daily rate equivalent, while his wife remains at home – on full, permanent contractual pay, mark you! – to look after their semi-legitimate offspring!

I was intent upon making a formal complaint to the senior management team about it this morning, but they were all cock-a-hoop about the latest communication from Kenny Cameron at the education offices. Apparently our chief adviser has been so impressed with the quality and breadth of our school's forward development plans that he's seen fit to commend them to Dangerous Dan Baxter, his chief education officer, who in turn has decided to present the documents to the senior directorate as a sterling example of a curricular-conscious school displaying streamlined management efficiency.

I couldn't believe that, either! Given the completely fallacious contents of Mr Pickup's forward development plan, to name but one, this revelation simply confimed Pickup's original claim when submitting his documentation: as long as the development plans exist, that's all that matters. The contents are irrelevant.

Nevertheless, I am beginning to wonder how long the deception can be maintained, and even Pickup blanched at news of the future widespread dissemination of his *magnum opus*. However, he soon regained his natural equilibrium once more and dismissed my concerns with a cheery wave.

'Forget it, Morris,' he scoffed. 'That's it been through the hands of a depute head, a headteacher, a chief adviser and a divisional education officer – and not one of the buggers has read it yet! And neither will anyone else – no matter how high up the ladder it goes. Wait and see!'

I shall.

Thursday

The usual air of pre-Christmas anti-climax hung over our sparsely populated school this morning, with only about 20% of pupils bothering to record a presence on this, the second-last day of term. Conversely, we had an unexpected *increase* in staff attendance in the unlikely person of Matthew Gordon.

'Good grief!' I exclaimed involuntarily as he thrust his head around the staffroom door this morning.

'Anyone seen George Crumley?' Matthew queried. 'Just to let him know I'm back.'

Speechless with disbelief, I pointed in the direction of the gents' toilet whither George had just departed. Strangely enough, Mr Pickup appeared unconcerned, even unsurprised, by Matthew's sudden return to health:

'Oh no,' he answered my enquiry after Matthew had followed Crumley into the lavatory. 'No surprise at all, Morris. It was either today or tomorrow, but he'd need to be in sometime to report on duty so he can certify himself fit to work and get off the sick register in time for the holidays. Then he'll go back on it after Christmas. It'll mean he can start his period of continuous allowable sick-pay all over again.'

'No!' I gasped in amazement. 'He wouldn't,' I shook my head from side to side. 'I mean, he couldn't. Could he?'

Pickup looked genuinely bemused by my question. 'Well, he just has, Morris. He just has ...'

Friday

A fairly disastrous conclusion to the term for yours truly, which leads me to think that a pre-Christmas, anticlimactic atmosphere is to be preferred to the more spectacular – and somewhat licentious – proceedings initiated by Mr Pickup this afternoon. Mindful of my indiscretions with the tea-urn at last year's staff Christmas lunch, I had certainly hoped that this year's event would pass off with little or no event. Alas, it was not to be.

To explain, Pickup had apparently been set athinking by my staffroom observation yesterday about the last days of term being a fairly dismal and unspectacular festive conclusion to the year – especially since we've been stopped from having a Christmas sevice lest we offend any of the multifarious ethnic groupings which comprise our current school population.

Secure in the knowledge that our pupil attendance rate this

afternoon would be in the region of 2%, Pickup had therefore decided to enliven our post-prandial staff gathering with the surprise engagement of a pair of female entertainers in their professional capacities of what I believe are known as Singing Telegrams!

Well, I'm all for a bit of light-hearted frivolity now and again, but to my mind this just went completely over the score. One minute I was sitting, slightly light-headed, enjoying my third or fourth glass of ginger wine, and the next thing I knew was that two scantily-clad – and extremely well-endowed – young ladies had burst into the staffroom dressed as policewomen – except I never recall seeing constabulary uniforms quite so revealing as those worn by our festive visitors!

Their tightly-fitting jackets were the closest they got to regulation issue. Both of them were also fully sheathed in sheer black basque corsetry which accentuated every natural curve – and a few unnatural ones as well – with which they had been endowed, whilst their normal disciplinary aids of truncheon and notebook had been supplemented by two extremely viscious-looking leather whips. High-heeled shoes, black stockings and – need I go on? – full sets of suspenders completed the outfits, both of them jauntily set off by a pair of black-checked hats with the inscription 'Firm Discipline Required' writ large across their foreheads.

Proclaiming their whistle-announced visit as a 'Christmas Raid', the two of them proceeded to serenade us with a few shrill carols, during which renditions they attempted to drape themselves alluringly around any male staff member – so to speak – who happened to be in their respective paths. Peter Chittick, needless to say, lapped it all up!

Well, as I say, I'm all for a bit of fun, but I certainly thought this went beyond the boundaries of good taste. A disapproving frown began to form on my face, but before I could put my thoughts into words, Pickup thrust himself in front of me, a party-hat askew his bald and ruddy features.

'What d'you think then, Morris?' he blew a party squeaker into my nose. 'You said the place could do with some festive cheer, didn't you?'

As cooly as I could, I indicated my disapproval of the whole affair, remarking most particularly on its unprofessionalism, and reminding him most forcefully of the headmaster's recent edicts.

'Oh, don't be such a wet fart, Morris!' he seemed annoyed by my remarks. 'It's just a bit of fun!'

'That's all very well Mr Pickup, but –' I was stopped short as

Pickup interrupted the carol singing and – to my horror – invited both of our singing courtesans to make my closer acquaintance!

Possibly as a result of Pickup's verbal chastisement describing me as a killjoy, or possibly as a result of rather more ginger wine than I cared to admit, I must have decided – lest I spoil the party for everyone else – to accept the briefest of kisses and a quick cuddle from each of our protruberant visitors.

As I welcomed the one called Inspector Dolores into my lap, I do remember thinking that this would be the worst possible moment for anyone of importance to witness the festivities. Anybody even remotely acquainted with the details of my career to date will not, of course, be surpised to learn that this was *exactly* the moment chosen by Mr Tod for one of his rare forays into the staffroom, accompanied – my heart sinks as I recall the scene – by Dangerous Dan Baxter, no less!

Silence descended upon the staffroom, with the sole exception of Peter Chittick who had failed to notice our new arrivals: his stringent vocal urgings to 'get stuck in there, Morris!' cut across the gathering like a knife, and almost created a worse impression than my own physical contortions in the corner. Almost. But not quite.

'Get your hands off that woman's leg, Mr Simpson,' Mr Tod's menace-laden voice scythed across the room. 'Excuse me, Mr

Baxter,' he turned to our visitor in furious embarrassment. 'As I was just saying outside, the senior management team have been *trying*,' – and I thought he emphasised the word 'trying' rather too strongly – 'to instil a greater sense of professionalism amongst the staff at Greenfield. Although with *some* people,' – and here he looked sternly at my dishevelled, lipstick-smeared countenance – 'I guess we might as well not bother!' With which closing and condemnatory remark he ushered Mr Baxter from the room.

It was difficult, given my recumbent and physically vulnerable position, to state my fulsome agreement with his policy of increasing the professionalism of our staff, and he probably wouldn't have stayed to listen anyway. Dolores must have sensed my dismay. Removing her hand from inside my shirt, she took out a notebook and licked her pencil instead.

'Never mind him, dearie,' she cooed in my ear. 'Shall I take his name for you?'

'That's all right,' I sighed wearily. 'I think I already know it.' Aggrieved at the injustice of it all, I simply requested that she remove her other hand from my knee, and hung my head with a sense of despair to which I am, by now, only too fully accustomed ...

January

Ashvale Private Health Clinic
(consultations by appointment)

Certificate of sickness

Name: Matthew Gordon
Nature of illness: rhinitis
Period of certifiable sick-leave: four weeks

Signed: B Fogarty, MD; PDSA

To the patient: please return remittance of £40 with this tear-off slip to Ashvale Clinic within 7 days of certification

As usual, it didn't take Morris long to bounce back from oppression. True, the incident with the strippogram girls had been a source of profound professional regret, but he felt sure that Mr Tod would fully understand the explanation he planned to offer in the new year – if only the man would come out of his study to meet his staff once in a while! Failing that, he reckoned that Mr Dick would stand up for him at the next meeting of the senior management team.

As it happened, both were forlorn hopes, but Morris wasn't to know that at the time. Instead, he looked forward eagerly to the first-year parents' night due for January, wherein he would be able to meet some of the parents of his favourite class and explain the details of the English department's new assessment scheme, which had apparently caused some confusion when the Christmas records of achievement had been sent home.

Based, as it was, on the Scottish 5–14 guidelines he spent some of his Christmas holidays preparing a useful information sheet which explained the achievement levels of 'A' to 'E' which children were expected to demonstrate throughout their first nine years of schooling. The only one of direct relevance at Greenfield, of course, was Level 'E', which was the standard to be expected of pupils at the end of their second year in secondary school, the previous four levels being related to incremental stages at primary school, beginning with Level 'A' at the end of primary two.

Naturally, for those parents used to more traditional forms of grading with letters A to E, this caused some confusion, but Morris reckoned it was nothing that a carefully-written information sheet couldn't sort out.

One teacher who was unlikely to be present at the first-year parents' evening was Matthew Gordon. As Mr Pickup had predicted, Matthew's recovery had been short-lived, and his subsequent lapse into yet another period of illness had coincided precisely with the opening of the new term.

Mr Crumley wasn't very pleased.

Monday

George Crumley is livid about the continued absence of Matthew Gordon from his geography department. True to the predictions outlined by Mr Pickup at the end of last term, Matthew's reappearance in school just before Christmas owed very little to a miraculous improvement in health, and a great deal to the man's awareness of holiday period sick-pay regulations. By the third day back after the new year, yet another certification of ill-health had been posted to the school office, and Crumley was once more presented with the impossible task of running a geography department with a succession of ill-assorted supply teachers.

'But how does he keep convincing his *doctor* that he's ill?' I queried Crumley at afternoon break. 'Can't *he* see through him, either?'

'Probably,' Crumley shrugged his shoulders in resignation. 'But he's gone private now.'

'Who? The doctor?'

'No, no,' Crumley explained. 'Matthew Gordon. He's abandoned his health-centre doctor and got himself a tame private consultant. Forty quid a consultation and this guy'll write you up with any disease you care to mention.' He screwed up his eyes in recollection: 'Rhinitis was the most recent one, if memory serves me right.'

'And what's that when it's at home?' I asked

'Common cold, according to my *Family Health Guide*,' Crumley informed me, '– but a particularly serious version.'

'So what does that mean in terms of Matthew's condition?' I asked.

'About another four weeks off bloody work, that's what it means!' George clenched his teeth. 'Unfortunately, I doubt if his condition'll be serious *enough*. Like terminal!'

Understandably, he seems very bitter about the whole affair.

I briefly offered sympathy and retired to my classroom for the last lesson of the day. Usually, this is a fairly unpleasant fifty minutes' worth, due in no small measure to the uninhibited behavioural capacities of Tommy McShane, but for the third lesson in a row he actually appeared interested in what we were doing and completed all of the written assignments which were set, as well as offering the first voluntary, sensible, and civil answer which I recall hearing from the boy in four years of secondary education.

It's all very worrying. I wonder what he's planning?

Tuesday

McShane's improved behaviour has been explained by the shock appearance of his elder sister, Rose, as my new cleaning lady!

'Hullawrerr, sur!' she greeted me as I walked in to collect some marking to take home at 4 o'clock. It was as if a ghost had walked over my grave, as horror-filled recollections of Rose's previous incarnations came to mind – she was in my first O grade repeat class some five years ago, and even came back to haunt me as an adult returner after that.

'Oh, gosh!' I stuttered in surprise 'Well – er – hullo, Rose?' I queried stupidly. 'What are *you* doing here?'

She gave me that dismissive look which I remember so well from our previous relationship, before thrusting out two mop-laden arms, shaking her ample girth from side to side whilst announcing that she was 'the bloody floor-show!', and asking me what I *thought* she was doing there!

As a teacher of many years' experience, I have always found it best to ignore sarcasm if at all possible: my patient request for a more accurate explanation led me to understand that, having remained idle since leaving school, Rose had at last located a source of part-time employment with Kleenup, our newly-privatised cleansing operatives. However, it appeared that industrial relationships were already somewhat soured, even at this early stage of Rose's employment.

'It's bloody slave labour, sur, so it is! Works out about fifty pee an hour, or sumthin' like that! And –'

'Please, Rose,' I interrupted her gently. 'There's no need to call me "sir" any more.'

'Oh?' she enquired.

'No, no. Mr Simpson will be just fine.'

'Right, sur,' she continued unawares. 'And, anyway, there's nae employment protection, or anythin' like that. We could all be out'n'r erses the morra if –'

'Yes, yes, Rose – I know,' I endeavoured to steer the conversation towards less controversial matters, such as the recent behavioural improvement of her sibling.

'Toammy?' she nodded firmly. 'That's right. Ah telt 'im ah wis wurkin' here now, an' if ah heard any beamers about him no' behavin' wi' the teachers then ah'd knoack his fuckin' brains out!'

'I see,' I gulped awkwardly, suddenly realising that young McShane's attitudinal improvement owed less to my behavioural modification attempts than I had thought.

What a shame. For once, I had really thought I was *getting* somewhere with a difficult pupil.

Wednesday

I don't think the cleanliness of my room is going to be improved to any great degree by Kleenup's latest recruit: I asked Rose today if she could see her way to leaving it looking less like a civic amenity site and more like a classroom, but I don't think she understood. Indeed, she spent most of her time banging a brush furiously up and down on the floor whilst berating her new employers as 'bloody chancers' and announcing that she was 'goanny get some action'!

Eventually, I asked her to leave because she was distracting me from my preparations for tomorrow night's first-year parents' evening – my room still looked in a terrible state, but I don't think Rose's continued presence would have made the slightest bit of difference anyway.

Thursday

First-year parents' evening. A wearisome occasion, made even worse by Mr Kelly's intractability during enquiries after his daughter's school progress.

'Brian Kelly,' he introduced himself in business-like fashion about half-way through the evening. 'Catherine's father. You're Mr Simpson, aren't you? I'd like to know how Catherine's doing in English.'

'Ah, yes – Catherine Kelly,' I invited Mr Kelly and his wife to sit down across the desk whilst I tried to remind myself what on earth their daughter looked like. 'She's – uh – she's doing fine, Mr Kelly,' I assured him sincerely, still playing frantically for time as I ran my eyes down the class list. 'She – uh – she certainly seems to enjoy English, and –'

'Oh yes?' his eyes narrowed. 'Any particular aspect of it?'

'Well – um – all of it, really,' I prevaricated once more.

'Drama?' he asked. Gratefully, I latched on to the clue at once.

'Oh yes, she *loves* drama,' I assured him. 'I mean, I know they *all* do at that age, but Catherine really enters into the spirit of –'

'That's strange,' he interrupted me. 'She's always *hated* drama up until now.' His eyes narrowed again. 'She's a very *shy* girl, our Catherine, you know ...'

Suddenly I knew the girl he was talking about: a wee mouse of a thing who's never opened her mouth since the day she came into my class!

'Ah, well yes,' I parried quickly, hiding my confusion. 'I know

that, of course, but although she doesn't take much part in the actual *performances* of the plays we read, I can certainly see she's taking it all in, Mr Kelly – I mean, her written work bears testimony to that,' I hurried quickly on to the more positive aspects of Catherine's classroom performance.

'Ah, yes,' he agreed. 'So she's getting on well with her compositions, then?'

'Free written expression? She certainly is, Mr Kelly.'

'And what does that mean?' he enquired earnestly.

'Free written expresion? Well, that's the name we give to –'

'No, I know that,' he replied testily. 'I meant, what does it mean if she's getting on well with it?'

I paused. 'Well, it means she's – uh – it means she's doing very *well* in it.'

'How well? How's she doing in relation to the rest of the class?'

'Ah well,' I began to explain, on slightly safer ground now. 'We don't actually *compare* them to each other these days, Mr Kelly. That would be norm-referencing them, and we feel that such an approach can be very demotivating to those at the lower end of the academic spectrum.'

'Sorry?' He looked confused.

'What we do,' I continued solicitously, 'is to judge each pupil against a set range of predetermined critera, so that when a child achieves those criteria, then he or she can be awarded credit for so doing.' I paused, and hoped he wouldn't ask any awkward questions.

'OK,' he agreed initially. 'I'll buy that one. So how's she doing then?'

'She's doing very well,' I ventured once more. I thought he was about to interrupt again, so quickly gabbled on to explain that already his daughter had 'achieved a level E in 5–14 terms.'

'A level E?' he shook his head in bewilderment. 'But Catherine always got straight A's in primary school!'

'Ah no, Mr Kelly,' I tried to soothe him. 'A level E in 5–14 is actually the standard of attainment she should have reached by the end of *second* year, not a norm-referenced performance indicator, and –'

'Oh, for God's sake don't start that educational claptrap again!' he broke out in frustration. 'If you think she's doing fine, then fine. But I've got my doubts, I don't mind telling you. As far as I can see she's at the same stage now as when she left Rockston primary, and half the time she spends in this place is a complete waste of –'

'Well, thank you very much for coming along tonight, Mr Kelly,' I swiftly looked at my watch, mindful of the three sets of parents waiting behind him. 'Any such general matters of school curriculum policy can certainly be referred to the senior management team if you wish, but for the moment, please be assured that I'm more than satisfied with Catherine's performance in English.'

'Oh all right,' he accepted the termination ungraciously, before adding a final, somewhat pathetic plea: 'So d'you think she'll get her Highers, then?'

Having reminded him that the examinations in question were over four years away, I nevertheless expressed fulsome confidence in his daughter's ability to achieve a large and varied clutch of examination passes at the highest level. He went away more than satisfied, and with any luck I won't be around when it comes time for the reckoning.

That's how to deal with them! To be perfectly honest, I think it's disgraceful when parents call one's professional judgement into question in that fashion. In my opinion, if I tell someone their daughter's doing well, then they should simply accept it, and be glad of the fact!

I was so annoyed that I forgot to hand him my 5–14 information sheet. Mind you, it was probably just as well: it would probably have been beyond him!

Friday

Mr Dick, our promotion-hungry depute head, is in seventh heaven! He spent all morning squeaking excitedly about the recently-received news that Dangerous Dan Baxter, our divisional education officer, has selected Greenfield Academy to be a pilot school for the regional staff development programme. Despite his surprise over the appearance of a strippogram at last term's staff Christmas party – an orgasmic event for which Mr Tod continues to blame *me*, of all people, instead of Mr Pickup, who had organised the damned thing – Mr Baxter nevertheless continues to view Greenfield as a source of dynamic educational innovation.

The biggest irony of all is his continued appreciation of Mr Pickup's ruddy forward development plan: this specious and wholly counterfeit document has acquired a glowing reputation which has simply served to confirm Pickup's original premise concerning such educational tomes, that they are always 'seen but never heard'. Or read, obviously.

And now Baxter wants to 'pull Pickup in to head-office on a secondment', as he puts it in the quasi-managerial prose so beloved of educational management these days. Pickup's assistance is, apparently, urgently required to provide in-service guidance on the construction of forward development plans for the integrated curriculum.

Knowing full well Mr Pickup's views on such educational casuistry, I expected a snort of laughter and a point-blank refusal when Mr Dick made the proposition. However, I had reckoned without the blatant self-interest which Pickup holds dearest to his heart:

'But of course, Mr Dick,' he jumped at the opportunity. 'More than ready to help out on that score. Integrated curriculum development's just my cup of tea, y'know ...'

My own speechless astonishment was in marked contrast to Mr Dick's enthusiastic acceptance of Pickup's willingness. But then – as I realised upon hearing Pickup's next question – Mr Dick knows the system all too well himself.

'So *how* long will I be out of school for?' Pickup raised an eager eyebrow.

'Ooh, about eight, nine –' Mr Dick began to muse, before Pickup interrupted in disappointed tone.

'Only eight days?' he queried. I'd have thought a project like this would take longer than that, Mr Dick.'

'Oh, not eight *days*, Mr Pickup,' Dick hastily corrected the wrong impression. 'Eight *weeks* was what I was thinking of. Unless you think it'll take longer, of course?'

Plainly, Pickup was finding it difficult to restrain himself, but he had the decency to do so until Dick had left the staffroom.

'A secondment!' he punched a victorious fist in the air. 'Hally-bloody-lujah!' he exploded in divine gratitude. 'Out of this stinking cesspit at last and into a comfy chair at regional offices! And this is just the start, Morris,' he waved a finger at my sagging jaw. 'Once I'm out, don't think they'll get me back in here without a bloooody struggle! A secondment for David Pickup!' he repeated, rubbing his hands together with ecstatic delight. 'Would you bloody believe it, Morris? Would you? Eh?'

Frankly, I still don't think I can.

February

STILL LIFE

Preparations for a secondment ...

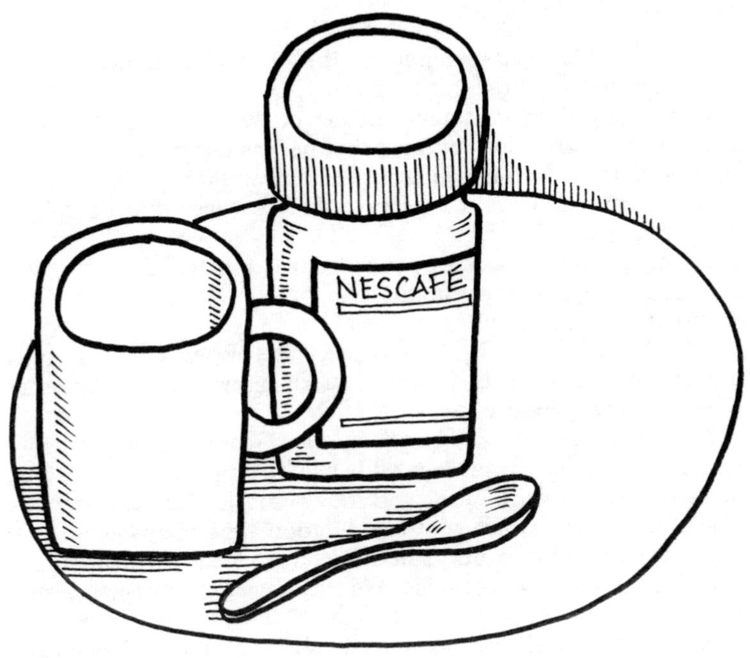

As David Pickup prepared for, and celebrated, his impending regional secondment, life at Greenfield Academy continued apace, in much the same vein as before.

Morris continued to experience a difference of academic opinion with Mr Kelly, whose worries over his daughter's progress were not restricted to a concern about her levels of attainment in English, as Morris was to discover during the month of February.

Also, whilst he had every sympathy with Rose McShane and her cleansing operative colleagues about their conditions of service, Morris was becoming genuinely distressed about the insufficient levels of hygiene which pertained in his classroom, and throughout the school. In his opinion, there was no longer any doubt about the matter: the place was becoming a health hazard.

And in the geography department, there was still the eternal absence of Matthew Gordon. It had all got too much for George Crumley, as Morris couln't help but notice one Monday morning in February.

Monday

George Crumley was banging his head off the staffroom wall when I arrived in school this morning.

I found it difficult to know whether he was laughing or crying, and closer investigation revealed that he was experiencing a similar emotional dichotomy himself. It was Mr Pickup who discovered the reason behind our principal teacher of geography's distressed state.

Gently prising a piece of paper from Crumley's clenched fist, he scanned the document in question.

'What is it?' I queried.

'Matthew Gordon's latest sick-line,' he whispered. 'Just arrived this morning, along with George's latest supply-teacher – another beanbagger, apparently.'

All became clear. Since October, poor George has yet to experience three consecutive days with a full complement of staff in his department owing to the tortuous – and innovative – succession of illnesses to which Matthew Gordon appears prone.

'So what is it this time?' I nodded down at the medical certificate which Pickup was reading, his eyes growing wide with disbelief.

'Urtucaria …' he scampered over to consult the staffroom dictionary. 'What the hell's –?' he muttered quickly through the pages, before announcing, triumphantly: 'Got it! Here you are, George! Nettlerash: that's what he's got this month. Would you believe it? Nettlerash!'

Crumley slumped against the wall and started to make quiet sobbing sounds. It was all rather pathetic, really.

Tuesday

One of the problems connected with being an assistant principal teacher of guidance is that one frequently has to defend colleagues against parents, even when not entirely sure of one's facts.

A case in point arose this morning, when Mr Kelly arrived without notice for an interview about his daughter's progress in mathematics.

'Oh!' his face registered dismay as I collected him from the entrance hall to take him back to my office. 'But you're Catherine's English teacher, aren't you? We met last month at parents' night.'

'Indeed, Mr Kelly,' I confirmed, recalling the interview with some discomfiture. 'But matters of enquiry about general academic progress outwith the format of parents' evenings need to be channelled through the guidance structure in the first instance and then taken up with the relevant subject department by the line-guidance principal, after due consultation with the rest of the guidance staff about the pupil's progress in other subject areas to discern if a pattern of any sort seems –'

He cut me short. 'But I just want to speak to her maths teacher about her maths,' he complained sharply. 'Mr Dunbar wasn't here at parents' night, so I wanted to clear up a few things. I don't *need* to speak to her guidance teacher!'

'Well, I'm afraid that would run contrary to the pastoral structure we have in place here at Greenfield Academy for parental consultations, Mr Kelly. And actually, I'm not Catherine's guidance teacher anyway.'

'No?'

'No. I'm fourth-year guidance actually, but Miss Honeypot's away on a course today about home/school links, and Mr Fraser's off with a virus. However, I've got Catherine's file here,' I patted the folder beneath my arm, 'and if there's anything which still seems unclear at the end of our interview, then I'm sure we can refer the matter to another guidance principal for further –'

He cut me short again. 'All right,' he sighed. 'Let's just get on with it.'

In short, as he explained back in my office, Mr Kelly's main concern centred on the methodology employed by the maths department in teaching junior classes. His principal complaint was that Catherine didn't seem to have been 'taught much maths since she came here. They just sit around in groups chatting to each other.'

'Ah, well that's their maths scheme,' I hastened to explain. 'Mr Dunbar's department uses a scheme which employs the discovery method.'

'The what?'

'Discovery method. The pupils learn about mathematical techniques by conducting investigations and drawing mathematical conclusions from them.'

'And who decides what the investigations will be about?'

'They do. It's all self-generated. There are tremedous motivational benefits when pupils decide for themselves what kind of work *they* wish to attempt.'

'I'm sure there are,' he raised both eyebrows in barely-concealed scepticism. 'So I'm right?' he continued. 'They never get *taught* anything?'

'No, not exactly, Mr Kelly,' I assured him. 'It's true that they seldom experience a whole-class lesson in the way you or I might remember them, but –'

'So I *am* right!' he repeated himself with conviction. 'Dunbar just wanders around the room chatting to them about the time of day?'

'No, no, no, Mr Kelly,' I tried to reassure him once again. 'Mr Dunbar would see himself as a *facilitator*, or an *enabler*, rather than a teacher in the old-fashioned sense of the word. His presence *facilitates* the learning objectives, and enables the children to discover mathematical truths themselves rather than being taught them in a narrow didactic manner. You see?'

Although I was getting slightly out of my depth, I think I must have said enough to satisfy him. At any rate, he announced his immediate intention of leaving and thanked me – rather brusquely, I thought – for my valuable time and for clarifying the picture with such precision.

I do wish that parents would leave education to us professionals.

Wednesday

Tommy McShane's recently improved behavioural standards continue to surprise me, and I'm sure it's not all down to the threats of physical retribution from his elder sister Rose, my new cleaning lady. The boy – until recently one of the most recalcitrant pupils in my fourth year class – appears to be taking a real interest in my English lessons, especially during our current theme study on death. It's all very rewarding: his enthusiasm's like a breath of fresh air.

Which is more than can be said for the atmospheric state within the school itself: I really do wonder if it's becoming a hygiene risk, owing to the appalling deterioration of cleansing standards since the appointment of Kleenup as our privatised contractors, and *their* subsequent appointment of Rose McShane as one of their employees. My room has never been so filthy, and the stench outside the third-year boys' toilets is simply appalling.

I made especial plea of Rose this afternoon to give my room a thorough 'going-over', but she pleaded lack of time owing to an imminent union meeting which she had called to discuss the cleaners' terms of employment with specific reference to worker exploitation.

'But Rose,' I questioned her, 'I thought your employers specifically forbade union membership in their employment terms.'

'Mebbe they do sur,' she shrugged. 'But they huvny come up against Rosie McShane yet! Wur goanny see some action against this bunch o' rapacious capitalist bastards!'

As she waddled forcefully out of the room, a mop in one hand and a duster in the other, I was forced to ponder the militancy of her new-found vocabulary – not to mention her chances of success, which I would rate as minor in the extreme. You don't take on companies like Kleenup lightly and get away with it.

Thursday

Mr Pickup's secondment to the regional offices starts next week. I still find it hard to believe that that they actually see Pickup as a serious provider of in-service advice on the matter of forward development planning.

Not so Mr Pickup.

'No sweat, Morris!' he responded confidently when I queried the possibility of nerves before his temporary move to the corridors of power. 'Secondments are a doddle!'

'Oh really?'

'Yes, really. Arrive whenever I like in the regional offices, go home when I fancy, and as long as I churn out the ocasional consulation paper, attend a few meetings here and there and display an ability to drink endless cups of coffee, then I'll be home and dry! And best thing of all – not a bloody kid in sight for miles!'

'But surely,' I countered, 'you'll have to give lots of talks to in-service groups?'

'No, no. *Talk*, Morris,' Mr Pickup corrected me. 'One talk. In the singular. Dan Baxter tells me he's got six in-service lectures lined up for me, but all with different divisional goupings. So I prepare one talk. Then give it six times.'

'And that's it?'

'Ah well, of course I have to evaluate the responses to the talk. And that's something that'll take a while, y'know, what with preparing the evaluation sheets, then modifying them in response to the feedback received.'

'And then modifying the talk, I suppose?' I agreed.

'Shouldn't think so,' Pickup shook his head dismissively. 'Nobody'll be at the same one twice, so there shouldn't be any need to go overboard on that score.'

'I see,' I murmured. 'So that's your secondment?'

'Uh-huh. Lots of meetings, plenty of coffee, prepare a lecture, and get everybody to fill in lots of evaluation sheets to show Dan Baxter how useful I'm being!'

It seemed a narrow view to me, but our discussion was cut short by the arrival of three strangers armed with clipboards who asked the whereabouts of the gents' staff toilet. My subsequent enquiries revealed them to be health inspectors investigating a mysterious tip-off about sanitary conditions arising from poor standards of cleaning.

I thought it best to warn Rose McShane this afternoon lest she get into trouble with her line-manager, but she seemed entirely sanguine about the health inspectors' arrival.

'As quick as that?' she nodded in apparent approval. 'Telt ye ah'd get action sur!'

'You're not telling me that *you* called them in, Rose? Are you?'

'Ask nae questions, sur,' Rose put a secretive finger to her lips. 'An' ye'll get telt nae lies ...'

Friday

Kleenup have lost the regional cleaning contract! Moved to action by the health inspectors' visit and a subsequent verbal report yesterday afternoon, the education authority announced a cancellation of the contract with immediate effect, due to sub-standard operative procedures. Interestingly enough, the contract has been re-awarded to the region's in-house contractor, which had initially provided the second-lowest bid in the original tendering procedure.

The new cleaners – in fact, they're the old cleaners, but there should be more of them – start next week, complete with union representation. And guess who they've got as their shop steward?

Actually, I'm sure that – given half-decent working conditions and a chance to prove herself – Rose will make good. Certainly, when she was a pupil I always found that she responded well to being given an extra modicum of responsibility. I said as much to Mr Pickup this afternoon, but he claimed – after he'd stopped laughing – that my recollections, and my spectacles, must have been coloured a rosier shade of pink than usual when I'd thought that one up!

However, he was more immediately concerned with a recent communication from Dan Baxter about the programme for his first days on secondment. Apparently Mr Baxter wants to go through Pickup's renowned forward development plan in some detail as he wishes to base the regional guidelines on Pickup's template.

'Blimey!' Pickup shook his head as he read the letter. 'I'd better get some guidelines together after all.'

'Ah-hah, Mr Pickup,' I reminded him. 'Be sure your sins will find you out! Looks as if Dangerous Dan's in danger of actually *reading* your development plan?'

'Maybe,' Pickup shrugged. 'And maybe not.'

'Here, Morris,' Joyce Honeypot interrupted us. 'What's this all about?' she announced a guidance enquiry of some import. 'It says in Catherine Kelly's file that you had an interview with her

dad on Tuesday and,' – she quoted briefly from my report – 'assuaged his concerns about Catherine's academic prowess with particular regard to mathematical investigative procedures.' Joyce wrinkled her nose. 'What the hell's that supposed to mean?'

'It's quite simple, Joyce,' I began to explain (she's a PE teacher), but before I could continue she was waving a letter angrily beneath my nose. 'And this too? Mr Kelly says here that he's decided to move Catherine from the school and place her in Abbotsgrange Academy.'

'Gosh!' I replied.

'Yes, gosh! Says he doesn't approve of private education in principle, but – and he says to "please tell Mr Simpson the following" – that despite the cost involved, he's decided – quote – "to *facilitate* his daughter's education by *enabling* her to be taught something once in a while'. Unquote. Throw any light on it, can you?'

'Well, I – I don't know what he's on about!' I gaped hopelessly. 'He certainly seemed uncertain about some of the teaching procedures in maths, but I assured him that Mark Dunbar ran a tight ship, and that –'

'Oh well,' Pickup interrupted. 'Catherine should be in good company over at Abbotsgrange. That's where Mark Dunbar's sons are as well, isn't it?'

'Mm,' nodded Miss Honeypot.

'You what?' I queried, incredulous. 'You don't mean –'

'Oh, certainly,' Pickup confirmed. 'Takes the Director's shilling for teaching here all right, but he's not likely to subject his *own* offspring to the institutionalised chaos of a state education. And especially not in maths! Over at Abbotsgrange Academy they're doing quadratic equations by the end of first year, and differential calculus by the end of second. And not a mathematical investigation in sight!'

Gosh! Talk about hypocrisy.

March

Greenfield Academy Option Choices

History	Geography
[illegible]	[illegible]
[illegible]	[illegible]
[illegible]	
[illegible]	
[illegible]	
[illegible]	
[illegible]	
[illegible]	
[illegible]	
[illegible]	
[illegible]	
[illegible]	
[illegible]	
[illegible]	
[illegible]	
[illegible]	
[illegible]	
[illegible]	
[illegible]	
[illegible]	
[illegible]	

As March drew to a close, Morris was saddened by the departure of Rose McShane from the team of school cleaners: despite her victory over pay and conditions with Kleenup, she had located a yet more remunerative form of employment as a conductress with the Parkland Bus Company, and Morris wished her well for the future, wondering if their paths would ever cross again. March is also, of course, the time for option choices at the end of second year: it is always a difficult time for principal teachers of geography and history, but this year George Crumley had the added burden of Matthew Gordon's absence – and its likely effect upon the popularity of his subject.

And – as if that wasn't enough – the month of March was to see a parental intervention concerning Crumley's marking standards with regard to the practical investigation of Standard grade geography. Alan Carswell had kept a relatively low profile since demitting office from the school board of Parkland High, but his daughter's presence in the fourth year at Greenfield Academy, plus Mr Carswell's commitment to ensuring that Janie received as high a grade as possible, meant that he was to figure once more in the Morris Simpson diaries.

It didn't really have a great deal to do with Morris, but for a variety of reasons he found himself caught up in the controversial discussions surrounding Janie Carswell's practical investigation grade. If only Mr Pickup had been on hand to lend some support ...

Monday

Strange as it may seem, I am missing Mr Pickup since he went on secondment to the regional offices: despite his rampant cynicism, I have often valued the companionship and advice which he provides, so it was with some pleasure that I accepted his telephone invitation to meet up in The Rockston Arms on Thursday evening to receive what he termed 'the low-down on some of the regional scandal'. I can hardly wait.

Meanwhile, life at Greenfield Academy continues in similar vein as before: confrontational and intensely depressing. George Crumley is still beset with the seemingly endless saga of Matthew Gordon's absence from his geography department (with a nervous ailment this month), and the latest addition to Crumley's sea of troubles concerned Mr Carswell's complaints about the mark awarded by the geography department for his daughter's practical investigation in Standard grade.

Unsurprisingly – given my previous delaings with the man – Mr Carswell rudely brushed aside my insistence that he channel any complaints through the appropriate guidance procedure (i.e. me).

'No way, Mr Simpson!' he remarked brusquely after barging round the school in search of Crumley. 'I want to speak to the man in charge of giving my daughter a level five for this!' he held aloft a closely typed sheaf of documents.

'But that can't be Janie's investigation, Mr Carswell?' I queried. Surely that should be in Mr Crumley's possession?'

'It's the copy I kept,' he snarled dangerously. 'And if Crumley won't improve the grade,' he threatened, 'I'll be sending it off to the SEB for consideration!'

Unfortunately, George Crumley chose just that moment to appear in the corridor, whereupon Mr Carswell continued his bitter tirade concerning the perceived slight against Janie's academic prowess. Crumley, of course, stoutly defended the award of a level five for the investigation and assured Mr Carswell that departmental marking standards had been fully moderated in the past by the exam board, but it cut no ice.

'Moderated my backside!' shouted Carswell in return. 'This investigation's worth at *least* a level two, if not higher, and you should know it, Mr Crumley!

It was all extremely embarrassing, but to his credit Crumley took it all in his stride and eventually pacified Mr Carswell by assuring him that he would, as a special favour, re-examine the work in question to see if any errors in the marking procedure might have arisen.

'And will you?' I queried him after Carswell had departed. 'Isn't it wrong to cave in to that kind of parental pressure?'

'Maybe so,' Crumley shrugged his shoulders, 'but you know me, Morris: anything for a quiet life. For a start, it doesn't really matter what grade I give the girl – there's very little chance of anyone checking up on it anyway. And secondly, the reason he's so uptight about it is probably because it's all his own work anyway. I'd hate to disappoint the old fart by giving him a level five.'

'You what!' my jaw dropped with astonishment. 'You mean *he* did the investigation –?'

Crumley looked puzzled at my surprise. 'Of course. Didn't you see that copy he showed us? *Very* mature sentence construction,' he emphasised. 'And beautifully typed – by Carswell's secretary, I'd wager – plus a set of accompanying photographs which looked as if they'd come straight out of a David Bailey manual. If you ask me, Carswell's been out with his Nikon auto-drive for the last six months getting photos like that.'

It seems outrageous, but Crumley assures me that such parental intervention is more common than anyone imagines. No wonder employers find it difficult to place much faith in our examination awards!

Sometimes I despair of the narrow range of interests displayed by the youth of today. Take my fourth year English class, for instance: when I was their age I relished nothing so much as the chance to go on extended cycle trips or occasional hillwalks, and most of my evenings were spent enjoying uplifting activities such as railway modelling or practising chess openings. And yet today when I asked them all to produce a written exposition of their favourite leisuretime activities, the most that any of them could muster was a half-page litany of electronic video games whose praises were sung in direct proportion to (a) the memory-drive required and (b) the list-price of each game under consideration.

Indeed the only elucidation I received from the entire exercise was the fact that Nintendo is not, contrary to my previous belief, a form of Japanese martial arts. Given the amount of time most of them spend on these trivial pursuits, it was hardly surprising that the literary quality of their descriptions was so appalling. Nevertheless, I felt it incumbent of me to point out to Alan McLeary that a comparison of his 'Game Gear' equipment with David Peck's 'Game Boy' equivalent would have been better phrased without the adjectival extravagances of 'shit-hot' and 'pretty crappy'. Such descriptive terminology, I have assured him,

is unlikely to find favour with Standard grade assessors, be they internal or not!

Ironically enough, it was the attempt of Tommy McShane to explain his wider interests which indicated that at least one of their number had widened his horizons beyond the electronic gimcrackery which so entrances his square-eyed colleagues. McShane's continuing interest in the subject of death and its associated trappings had led him to compose a surprisingly fulsome document explaining his recent survey of local graveyards and crematoria. Taken in conjunction with his recent attempts at poetic expression on the nature of the hereafter – somewhat immature, but laudable in intent – it would appear that Tommy McShane has at last found an interest in life. Or death, rather.

I wonder where it will all lead?

Wednesday

George Crumley's troubles are multiplying on a daily and exponential basis.

Today's distress stemmed from Mr Dick's release of the second-year option choice figures for next year. The continued inability of the geography department to provide a proper timetable owing to the constant absence of Matthew Gordon has led to a fairly major imbalance in that 104 pupils have chosen history as a third year option compared to 19 for geography!

The history department is cock-a-hoop, as you might well imagine – Martin Henderson was to be seen in one of Crumley's geography rooms with a measuring tape this morning – and I couldn't help but feel sorry for George as I watched him reading the list of pupls who had opted for geography. It didn't take long.

'Well George,' I tried a consolatory pat on the back, 'I suppose you can understand parents being uncertain about geography if their kids have had PE supply teachers for the subject all year long. But never mind: maybe once Matthew's better you'll be able to provide a proper timetable for them?'

'My God!' Crumley looked horrified. 'No way, Simpson. The longer that useless bastard's away the better. I mean, if he'd actually been *teaching* any of them the figures would've been even worse!'

Thursday

Aside from the pathetic attempts of my first year to catch me out with some April Fool tricks at period one (I refused to compromise my dignity by playing along) this was a tremendously exciting morning: there was a letter awaiting my arrival at school from a Mr Downside in the regional offices. In it, he explained that he was an area co-ordinator for 5–14 developments and, having heard about some of my guidance work, he wondered if I'd be interested in joining a regional working party on pastoral liaison between secondaries and their associated primary schools.

I was over the moon, I don't mind admitting it, and could hardly wait to break the good news to Pickup at our meeting tonight. And when I got to the Rockston Arms, things got even better: as soon as I walked in the door, who should I see but Matthew Gordon! There he was, knocking back one drink after another and looking nothing less than the picture of perfect health. I thought to myself that if this was a man suffering from a nervous complaint, then my name wasn't Morris Simpson. His presence in the pub would be just the kind of evidence Mr Dick would need to alert the region to the man's work-evasion tactics, and I looked forward to passing on the necessary information in the morning.

And to cap it all, not long before Pickup arrived I caught the distinctive and peremptory tones of Alan Carswell drifting across from the lounge bar. Fortunately, he couldn't see me, but I could watch *him* in the mirror – and listen as well – as the man unfolded the most amazing tale of deception I'd ever heard! In short, he was boasting to one of his business cronies about how he had managed to 'sort out Janie's practical investigation grade', a narrative which he concluded by proclaiming that he'd 'paid good money for that investigation' and that he was consequently unwilling to see such an investment wasted.

'Thirty quid is thirty quid in anyone's language,' he concluded loudly. 'And if it was worth a level one *last* year for Brian McNeill's son, then there's no way I'm settling for anything less than a level two from that bunch of chancers,' he declared angrily.

I couldn't believe my ears, and was agog with excitement when Mr Pickup arrived. Sadly, he seemed litle interested to hear my evidence of the educational criminality raging on the other side of the whisky gantries, and instead spent the first half-hour of our meeting telling me about the recently-announced series of early retirements from the regional offices as well as from schools across the entire region.

'You wouldn't believe it, Morris!' he shook his head with incredulity. 'They're chucking money around like there's no tomorrow.'

'How d'you mean?' I queried.

'An early retirement here, a golden handshake there. Half the bloody directorate's for the off, as well as any naff teachers they've been wanting to get rid of for donkeys! It's the biggest sodding clear-out,' he reminded me somewhat indelicately, 'since you had that major bout of diarrhoea after the Christmas party two years ago!'

Pickup then went on to suggest, in even cruder terminology, that his scatalogical recollection and comparison might be considered particularly appropriate given the nature and quantity of personnel about to be jettisoned from the regional employment register, but I wasn't prepared to listen to his carping any more. Rather, I hastened to alert him to the exciting news about my own potential secondment to the 5–14 working party and drew out my letter in proud evidence of the fact.

That certainly stopped him in his tracks. His eyes widened and I thought, for once, I'd actually rendered him speechless. Alas, however, his face soon creased into a particularly childish grin, after which he placed an avuncular arm across my shoulders.

'Morris,' he spoke softly. 'Have you checked the credentials of that letter fully?'

'Well, I don't need to,' I responded testily. 'It's on regional notepaper, and –'

'Morris,' he interrupted quietly again. 'Have you checked the date today? And at the top of that letter?

My eyes darted suspiciously to the letterhead, and back to Pickup once more.

'The – uh – first of April by the look of it,' I muttered hesitantly, my heart beginning to sink in realisation.

'And the name?' he beseeched me. 'Mr Downside? Don't tell me you didn't get it, Morris? Don't tell me that?'

'Oh,' I nodded sadly, looking up at him for confirmation. 'Mr – uh – Downside, I presume?'

'Yes, Morris,' Pickup confessed, apparently embarrassed that he'd had to explain the nature of his April Fool in such detail. 'Just a wee joke, old son. Actually, I didn't think it'd get past first base, to be honest, what with the name and the contents. I mean, surely you didn't believe they'd ever want *you* to be on a regional working party?!'

My lips hardened in resolve and I looked pointedly into his

eyes. 'Stranger things have happened, Mr Pickup,' I spoke grimly. 'Stranger things have happened.'

And to think I ever missed him.

The evening fell a litle flat after that revelation, and I even forgot to tell Pickup about Alan Carswell's gross deception with regard to Janie's geography grading. But wait till I tell Mr Crumley: it should certainly strengthen *his* hand in the argument.

Friday

Alas, my hopes for a couple of brownie points from the information gathered about Matthew Gordon were dashed by his arrival in school this morning. His appearance caused little surprise to George Crumley, who reminded me that, as this was the last day before the Easter holidays, it was perfectly in line with all expectation and previous record of behaviour that Matthew should show up today.

'Holiday pay. Remember?' he tapped a finger to the side of his nose.

I tutted and shook my head in disapproval before acquainting him with my even hotter news of Alan Carswell's overheard conversation. Strangely enough, Crumley seemed more embarrassed than angered.

'Blimey,' he commented. 'No wonder he was so sure it was higher than a level five if he bought it as a level one from last year.'

'Yes,' I agreed, 'but it's disgraceful, isn't it? What d'you think we can do about it?'

'Do about it?' Crumley looked puzzled. 'Well, first of all I'd better it changed to a level one pretty smartish, hadn't I?'

'What?! But surely you can't – ?'

'Of course I can. I'll just tell Carswell that it was a clerical error or something, and that we're terribly grateful to him for drawing it to our attention. Damned sight better than admitting we'd be as well sticking a pin in a board when it comes to marking these practicals.'

It was a fairly frank admission. I just hope the exam board never gets to hear of it.

April

Parkland Gazette Private Sales

FOR SALE: Alsation with friendly nature and large appetite. Loves children. £50. Tel Rockston 46793
FOR SALE: Geography practical investigation - Grade 1 awarded for previous 2 years. £35 ono. Tel Parkland 36980
FOR SALE: Crash examination tuition from experienced English teacher: £15 per hour, negotiable. Also pastoral guidance available or chess lessons. Tel Freeman 862570

Whether anyone within the regional offices ever *did* read David Pickup's forward development plan will remain, for ever, a matter of conjecture.

Pickup certainly believed, as a result of several in-house conversations, that the document had been read by Martin Woolf – a senior member of the directorate – and proclaimed that the man had indeed realised how spurious had been the basis of Pickup's rise to prominence. However, according to Pickup, it had been deemed too late to do anything about his mistaken promotion without embarrassing the region over the matter so the whole affair had been hushed up. Other, less charitable, observers were more direct: George Crumley, for example, contended that in-house personnel such as Martin Woolf would be 'so used to reading piles of shite that they probably couldn't recognise a genuine dollop when they saw one.'

For his part, Morris Simpson – as ever willing to view events in their kindliest light – reckoned the most likely outcome was that the document had simply been lost, like so many before and so many after, in the amorphous wastes of paper and middle-management which inhabited the regional offices.

In any case, of more immediate distress to him than the chicanery surrounding Mr Pickup's temporary promotion was the absolute deceit being practised by internal assessors of nationally graded examinations. At least, as April drew to a close, he was comforted by the annual onset of those more traditional – and to his mind, more reliable – forms of national assessment.

Monday

Exams ahead! Although school examinations today depend upon a greater degree of internal assessment than hitherto, the current preparations for Standard grades and Highers do at least give our senior students some experience of the academic rigours to which they will be subject should they go on to further education or university. And – as I discovered last month – the continued existence of such external examinations is to be welcomed, given the criminality which surrounds the preparation and marking of some pupils' internally assessed presentations!

To be honest, the likelihood of any of my fourth year guidance group remaining within the groves of academe must remain extremely limited: for the majority of them a 90 minute session with a video-game console remains the summit of intellectual aspiration. It was with such thoughts in mind that I delivered my annual pre-study-leave 'pep-talk' to my own class this afternoon.

'Now, over the next few weeks,' I explained gravely, 'you'll all have the opportunity to devote yourselves to private study without the neccessity of attending classes.'

'Yoahhh!' David Peck punched a clenched fist in the air.

'Right on, sur!' Alan McLeary raised both thumbs in friendly salutation whilst the rest of the class displayed celebratory responses of a similarly enthusiastic nature.

I suspected that their joy was unlikely to be attributable to the enhanced opportunities for last minute swotting, and my subsequent straw-poll of their intended revision plans soon proved my assumption correct.

Billy Cox, for example, informed me that he would by all means have a 'quick look' over his English notes on the night before his Standard grade exam, but that otherwise he had several sessions booked at the Rockston ice-rink which would take up most of his 'spare time' over the next few weeks. David Peck and Alan McLeary, in turn, recognised the imminent opportunity of improving their 'Sonic Mario scores', or something like that, whilst Rothesay Kyle needed to have the term 'revision' explained to her in words of fairly spartan syllables.

'So ye mean wur supposed tae read a' thae books'n'stuff *again*?' she questioned me, incredulous.

'That's right, Rothesay,' I confirmed. 'To make sure you can answer any questions which might come up on them.'

Her response was not encouraging. 'Christ, it wis borin' enough readin' them *wunce*!' she exclaimed. 'Ah'm no' readin' them *again*!'

I called a halt to the generally chorused murmur of agreement which began to swell around the classroom by explaining to them, in the severest tones I could muster, that these exams represented their best chance of forging a decent path into adulthood and full employment.

'Some of you are leaving school this summer,' I reminded them, 'and you're going to find out in the big wide world that you'll need to *work* to achieve a living! And what's more, you'll need to demonstrate a maturity and an adult understanding which seems sadly lacking in most of you.'

As if to prove the point, Billy Cox interrupted my little homily by jumping from his seat with an extremely vulgar exclamation of delight – the result, I soon gathered, of his achieving a hitherto uncharted score on the hand-held video-game console with which he had been amusing himself beneath his desk for the previous fifteen minutes.

I confiscated it at once, of course, and issued a punishment exercise for the gross profanity which he had just broadcast across the classroom, but it depressed me intensely to realise that pupils like these were about to finish eleven years of compulsory education.

Education for *what*, I wonder?

Tuesday

If I find the attitude of certain pupils upsetting, it's nothing to the gore which rises within me when I contemplate teachers like Matthew Gordon. Amazingly enough, our hypochondriac colleague has at last completed a full week of teaching subsequent to his return after the Easter break – the first full week since he joined us last October. Imagine my incredulity, however, upon hearing him explain that today would be his last day in attendance for the next fortnight.

'So you *know* you're going to be ill for the next two weeks, Matthew?' I questioned him cautiously.

'No, no,' he explained brightly. 'I've *had* the illness already.'

'Oh?'

'Yes. Over the Easter holidays, unfortunately. Another dose of that viral complaint I had just before Christmas.'

'I see,' I answered. Actually, I didn't, and Matthew must have noticed my uncertainty.

'So if I was ill during the holidays, then it means I didn't get my holidays,' he explained helpfully. 'And under our conditions of service, then I'm entitled to an equivalent period of leave in lieu.'

I gasped at the audacity of the man. 'But what about your pupils?' I asked him. 'They've barely seen seven days of you since you started here, and they're due to sit their exams next month.'

'Well I think it would've been counter-productive to report to school when I was suffering from serious illness, Morris,' he frowned. 'And as for their exams, well I'll be back in a fortnight for some last minute revision. Won't I?'

I nodded quietly in surrender. He had left the staffroom before I thought to remind him that his certificate pupils would all be away on study leave by then. But I suspect he already knew that.

Wednesday

Matthew Gordon absent, as predicted. My annoyance at the situation erupted when I received a 'please-take' from Mr Dick to cover for Gordon's geography class at period 3 this morning.

Fortunately, the class was used to working on its own by now, so I spent the entire lesson in retributive mood composing a letter to the divisional education officer complaining in the strongest possible terms about the appalling abuse of the absence system perpetrated by teachers like Matthew Gordon. And what's more, I posted it this afternoon!

Now we should see some action!

Thursday

Tommy McShane's continuing obsession with death is beginning to make itself felt in other areas of school life, apart from the increasingly morbid submissions he presents within my English classroom.

This week alone, I have been in receipt of five guidance queries about the boy, the latest of which came from Miss Tarbet of home economics. She wanted to know why McShane had felt it necessary to design a cake-decoration which portrayed a graveyard complete with chocolate-bar tombstones and *in memoriam* inscriptions outlined in filigree sugar-icing. I urged patience and understanding, assuring her it was 'just a phase' which McShane is going through. Prior to this, however, I had just spent several minutes in earnest conversation with Mr Sharp of biology, who in turn had just spent several minutes with McShane, explaining that a knowledge of the average rate of corpse disintegration after burial was a fact unlikely to be required of him in his forthcoming Standard grade exam.

'What's *wrong* with the boy?' Sharp demanded. 'I've met some weirdos in my time, Simpson, but this one takes the biscuit!'

I defended McShane to the best of my abilities, urging Mr Sharp to look on the positive side of McShane's vastly improved behavioural attitudes since his new-found interest, and pointing out – to him and Miss Tarbet in turn – that these kind of cross-curricular references could look very impressive if we are ever to be honoured by a visit from Her Majesty's Inspectorate!

Friday

Once again, I despair of the unprofessional attitudes displayed by my colleagues. Having just finished my lunchtime cheese sandwiches, I was dismayed to notice Mr Crumley enter the staffroom with news of some disciplinary unrest in the fourth-year boys' common room, which also happens to be in incidental use as Peter Chittick's English classroom for the rest of the day.

'Looks like they're intent upon celebrating the end of their academic tenure here,' he announced, in reference to the impending commencement of study-leave. 'When I walked past it was beginning to look like a Kashmir market – and smell like one as well!'

Amazed that walking past was *all* he had seen fit to do, I nevertheless held my silence as Crumley unfolded further sordid details of his voyeuristic activities.

'There's Brian McNeill running a poker school in one corner, while David Boyd and Graham Taylor are organising a tag wrestling match in the other. Not to mention the game of dares that was going on at the front of the room!'

'Oh?' enquired Mr Dunbar of maths. 'Like what?'

'Ah, usual stuff,' Crumley shrugged his shoulders. 'Unscrew a few light bulbs, chuck a few water bombs out the window, that kind of thing. Oh!' he suddenly jerked his head in recollection, 'and the last I heard as I came away was Billy Cox daring Alan McLeary to urinate in the wastepaper bin!'

Dunbar pulled a face. 'Yeugh! That's going a bit far, isn't it?'

'Mmm,' Crumley nodded in agreement as he sifted through the contents of his pigeonhole. 'Don't think they would, actually. Still, maybe somebody should go up there and check it out,' he mused absent-mindedly as he threw a fistful of documentation into the staffroom litter bin. After which he sat down!

My jaw dropped at such an open abdication of responsibility. However, before I had time to put my thoughts into words Mr Dunbar had suggested the rescue mission fall to Peter Chittick, on the grounds of it being his classroom. Unfortunately, Chittick's every ounce of concentration was intent upon the manual dexterity required to increase his score on the hand-held video game which I had confiscated earlier in the week from the selfsame Cox.

'Canny go!' he shook his head distractedly. 'I'm just on level six – first time ever! Monica?' he threw the suggestion across to Miss Cunningham before turning his whole attention back to the excitable toy in his hands.

'No way!' she asserted her position forcefully. 'That's a guidance job. Joyce?' she turned to Miss Honeypot lounging in the corner.

'I'm first-year guidance,' she drew strongly on her cigarette. 'Should be you, shouldn't it, Morris?' she arched her eyebrows in my direction.

Having followed the conversation with growing disbelief, I was speechless for a moment. 'Uh – well, yes,' I eventually shook myself back to full consciousness. 'I mean, of course I will.' And I did.

Needless to say, I was too late. McLeary, partly surrounded by a crescent of grinning and smirking adolescents, was in the process of zipping up his trousers when I arrived in Room C6.

'Sur!' shouted David Peck triumphantly. 'Cleary's peed in the bin!'

My intended immediate action of getting McLeary to empty the bin before we went any further was abandoned when I realised that Chittick's standard-issue metal receptacle had been recently replaced by a fine wicker basket, which had proved less than watertight during McLeary's outrageous performance. Instead, I sent Simon Park for a mop and immediate janitorial assistance, and then I turned to McLeary.

Before I could open my mouth, his eyes were open wide, his hands outspread before me. 'It wisny me, surr. Ah didny dae nuthin'!' he pronounced – the picture of abject innocence before I

drew attention to his dishevelled clothing and the seeping evidence before my eyes.

'McLeary!' I spoke forcefully, and in my severest tones. 'You are nothing more than a savage! In fact, you're *worse* than a savage! You are positively disgusting, and a disgrace to this school.' Amazingly, my condemnatory description appeared a source of pride to the loutish oaf! He grinned sheepishly, so I chose another tack.

'Why, McLeary?' I pleaded, wrinkling my nose in distaste. 'Why? What on earth would make you *do* such a thing?'

McLeary shrugged his shoulders before nodding his head in the direction of Billy Cox. 'It wis him. He made me do it, sur.'

I couldn't believe it. 'You *what*? Billy Cox *made* you do it? Made you –?'

'Aye, sur. It wis his idea. He made me,' the accusation was repeated.

I smote my head and put McLeary on an immediate exclusion order. Admittedly, his impending study leave will make this less of a punishment than it might otherwise have been, but it will certainly appear on his school records, much to his distress I would imagine.

Having cleared the classroom and withdrawn common-room rights for the rest of the term (again, less of a punishment than I'd have liked it to be, given the time of year), I was intrigued to notice the quiet and solitary figure of Tommy McShane reading a book in the furthermost corner. He appeared aloof and distant from the unsavoury shenanigans which had preceded my arrival, so I went over to congratulate him on his improved behaviour of late. I always feel that positive reinforcement is such an important weapon in the guidance teacher's armoury.

'Well done, Tommy,' I ruffled his hair. 'Good to see you keeping away from trouble like that.' He raised his eyes, briefly acknowledging my presence before returning to his book.

'Um – what's that you're reading?' I interrupted again.

Once more, he raised his eyes briefly, darkly, before raising the tome from the desk, whereupon I was greeted by the somewhat salutory title of his chosen reading material: *The Embalmer's Handbook*.

'Oh. Um. Very nice, very nice,' was the only immediate comment which came to mind. 'Very nice indeed.'

In retrospect, it seemed a fairly useless response, and I began to sympathise with Mr Sharp and Miss Tarbet. McShane's behaviour *is* all rather unsettling. To be honest, he gives me the shivers.

May

In a professional sense, the month of May had always been one of mixed emotions for Morris Simpson, and this year was no exception. As the academic session moved into its final spasm, a succession of events took place to herald the end of term, as well as to mark the departure of senior pupils for the outside world. As usual, a leavers' disco had been arranged and, as usual, Morris had volunteered for stewardship duty on the night in question.

Nevertheless, despite the excitement surrounding those pupils who were leaving school, preparations still required to be made for next year's continuing population of Greenfield Academy. By now, of course, Morris had fallen into a regular pattern of lesson provision for most classes, so the task was less time-consuming than it used to be. Alas, the same could not be said for Martin Henderson: as will become apparent, the seemingly endless amendments of the syllabus for Standard grade history had brought a whole set of unwelcome and external pressures to bear upon Martin. And he wasn't very happy about it.

For Morris, however, the end of May was a generally relaxed time of year, especially with the English examinations out of the way so that he could devote more time to his guidance responsibilities, particularly the logistical arrangements concerned with putting 38 fourth year pupils out on work-experience placements.

And, of course, the end of May would see the return of Mr Pickup to daily classroom life. Morris was looking forward to the reunion, as his diary for that month will reveal.

Monday

Mr Pickup is due back from his secondment on Friday of this week: he claims to have enjoyed his time in the regional offices formulating strategic development plans, but I still feel that his real vocation lies in the classroom. Even though he would never admit it, I know he likes working with young people far too much to ever think about abandoning the chalkface altogether.

And I have to admit that I miss him. For instance, I know he would have been a useful source of advice when I was trying to line up my fourth-year guidance group with some last-minute work experience positions today. So far it has proved geographically impossible to fulfil Billy Cox's request for a 'five day spell at the Nintendo factory', given its eastern Asian location, and the boy seemed genuinely bemused that the best I could manage was a week-long offer as a counter assistant in Rockston Electrics. David Peck, meanwhile, showed the first glimmer of interest I can ever remember from the boy when he requested a placement with the Royal Mail as a postman – or postperson, perhaps I should say in these egalitarian times. Anyway, it soon emerged that the sole reason behind this enthusiasm was his consideration that the 'postie aye finishes at lunchtime', a clocking-off period which would allow him to spend the afternoons of his work-experience in the leisure-orientated environs of Rockston ice-rink, or even the local bookies!

And as for Tommy McShane, I am still considering the advisability or otherwise of sending him on his requested five day placement with Mr Johnston, the local undertaker. I know that I've defended the boy's somewhat morbid interest in death as being infinitely preferable to the frequently anti-social behaviour of his colleagues, but McShane's relentless investigations into the hereafter have begun to worry me slightly. In the end, I have relented in the hope that the experience teaches him there is nothing glamorous about his enthusiasm and then perhaps he can get it out of his system. He starts next week.

Tuesday

Martin Henderson, our acting principal teacher of history, is less sanguine than I had imagined about the prospects for next year's extraordinarily large intake of pupils wanting to sit history at Standard grade, as I discovered during the lunch hour today.

'It's bloody impossible,' he shook his head over a bundle of paperwork on the staffroom coffee table.

'Having trouble accommodating all your extra pupils, Martin?' I queried. 'Surely that's a nice kind of problem to have these days?'

'God, no!' he explained brusquely. 'That's the least of my worries. It's the bloody exam board that's making life impossible.'

'Oh? But I thought they'd responded to all the criticisms about Standard grade to make the exam more appropriate for –'

'Indeed they have!' he nodded his head grimly. 'So that this year we're still preparing them for the original arrangements. And next year we're preparing them for the amended arrangements.'

'So what's the problem?' I queried.

'And the year after that they're changing the whole bloody caboodle again so it's a completely *new* set of arrangements!' his voice shook with frustration. 'Honest to God, Morris, I don't know whether I'm coming or going! I'm supposed to be organising a departmental plan of work for the next three years – and every year's different! I feel as if I'm running around like a headless bloody chicken, I can tell you!'

I expressed general sympathy and – after assuring him that in no way did he resemble a headless chicken – I quietly excused myself.

Personally – and I would never say this to Martin – I felt he was being a little unfair towards the examination board, who are only trying to respond to the submissions which they receive from teachers across the land. Maybe Martin should try having a little empathy for them: I thought that's what history was supposed to be all about these days, anyway!

Wednesday

Martin Henderson's bitterness had grown to unmanageable proportions by this morning's break. As well as the troubles he has experienced in trying to organise next year's syllabus and timetable arrangements, Martin learned this morning that Sandra Denver, the principal teacher for whom he has been acting up during the past four years, is due to return from her staff tutor secondment next month, a full ten weeks earlier than originally scheduled ...

'They've done it again!' he shook his head in disbelief at learning of the news in this morning's staff bulletin. 'The bastards've done it again!'

'Done what?' I looked across the staffroom.

'Sent Sandra Denver back just before the holidays!'

'Well isn't that good, Martin?' I questioned him. 'Surely that'll mean you can liaise with her about next year? Take some of the weight off your shoulders?'

'And some of the bloody salary as well!' he cursed angrily. 'That's three times on the trot she's come back from an absence just before the holidays – last two times after her ruddy maternity leaves, and now –'

'Well, she could hardly have organised the ending of her own secondment the same way you claim she organised her pregnancies, now could she?' I tried to reason with him.

'No, I'm not saying that she did,' Martin accepted. '*This* time it's the bloody region saving themselves dosh again. If she'd gone on to the end of her secondment term she'd have still been on her PT salary, and so would I, for acting up. This way, I'm bumped down to APT level again, and Sandra waltzes in when all the work's been done ready for next year, not having done a hand's turn towards it! Honestly – she's worse than Matthew Gordon!'

Which reminded me that I hadn't heard of our school-phobic geography teacher for some weeks now.

'That's right,' Martin nodded in acknowledgement. 'George has finally got rid of him.'

'You mean he's been sacked?' I began to think my letter to the divisional education officer last month must have had some effect after all.

'God, no!' Martin laughed scornfully at the suggestion. 'You don't sack teachers like Matthew Gordon.'

'But he's the most blatant case of work-avoidance I've ever –'

'Yep,' Martin accepted happily. 'So the region's still sharing him round. Compulsory transfer – he's gone back to Freeman Secondary, where he started out. We'll probaly get him back again in about five years' time, I'd think.'

Unbelievable. And to think he's still on full salary as well. At least I won't have the daily frustration of seeing his name on the staff absence list any longer, not now that Freeman Secondary have got him back. And they're welcome to him!

Thursday

This evening was the occasion of the leavers' disco which Mr Dick organised for members of the fourth, fifth and sixth years who are due to leave school at the end of June.

Actually, it was quite interesting to meet up again with some of those pupils who have already departed our educational ministrations without official sanction: our senior classes have an attendance rate of approximately 25% at present – on a good day – and I feel quite strongly that we should be making more stringent attempts to ensure that our leavers receive their full quota of compulsory education during these valuable final weeks.

Indeed, I was given pause for thought along those lines as I looked out over the seething dance floor and realised that these youngsters were about to enter the world of adulthood. Apart from the work-experience which I am organising for some of them, I really wonder how well-prepared they are. Tonight, for instance, very few of them had the slightest idea of how they plan to occupy their time in the weeks, months and years subsequent to their departure, and as far as this evening was concerned I found myself completely unable to engage in serious conversation with *anyone* about their future.

Mr Dick, for example, set a shocking example of irresponsibility by engaging in a series of lewd and libidinous dance routines with several of the more attractive sixth year girls and it was little surprise that the more impressionable pupils took their lead from our depute's lechery. Graham Taylor and Carolyn Barker, in particular, spent much of the evening locked in passionate embrace whilst Billy Cox and Rebecca Ritchie put on a floor show which at one point looked set to travel well beyond the bounds of simulated erotic frenzy with which it had started. Luckily, the disc-jockey noticed just how excited young Cox appeared to be getting and changed the music tempo with only moments to spare.

Most unnerving of all, however, was the romantic bonding which seemed to spring up between Alan McLeary and Rothesay Kyle, of all people! These two, so long the bane of my professional life in both academic and behavioural terms, spent the entire evening in the centre of the dance floor, their respective tongues down each other's throats and their hands making

exploratory fumblings around and within the most intimate areas of personal body-space. It was all too much for me and I decided to put a stop to it as soon as possible. Self-consciously edging my way on to the dance floor and firmly refusing the entreaties of several fourth-years to 'waggle it about a bit, sur,' I eventually located myself next to Alan and Rothesay.

'Right, you two,' I hissed quietly. 'That's way over the top for a school dance. Disengage yourselves now!'

A loud slurp, the sound of suction contact being broken, escaped McLeary's lips before he eyed me with evil suspicion.

'Whit?' he curled a lip uncomprehendingly. 'Dis-en-*whit*?'

'Disengage yourselves,' I repeated. 'Separate from each other. What you're doing here's quite disgusting, and I'm sure your parents would be absolutely –'

McLeary's sneer turned to one of contempt. 'Aw, get tae fuck, sur. Wur sixteen. We kin dae whit we like,' he tossed in my direction before returning his full attentions to the gaping demands of Rothesay's salivating orifice. Furiously, I raised my hands to their respective collars to initiate the separation by force if necessary, but was immediately thrown off balance by the onrush of a 'leavers' conga' which had been recently initiated by the disc-jockey. Suddenly, I found myself thrust into the lead-position and, unwilling to spoil the party for everyone else, I abandoned my attempted role as chaperone for the evening, swung my left leg in the air, and resolved to speak to McLeary tomorrow instead.

Anyway, there's nothing I like better than a good-going conga and – even if I say so myself – I think I made a pretty good job of being its leader (though I'm not so sure the headmaster will agree when he sees his study tomorrow). But as far as I was concerned it brought an element of clean and wholesome fun into what would otherwise have been a somewhat sordid evening. And a jolly good thing too.

My bus trip home was enlivened somewhat by the presence of Rose McShane as its conductress! She seems to have taken to her new job like a duck to water, and I was particularly impressed by the ease with which she quelled a potential disturbance by some of our fourth year boys who were on the same bus home. I had been going to have a few quiet words with them myself, but Rose's more confrontational approach seemed, on this occasion, to pay dividends.

Friday

Mr Tod was, indeed, most displeased about the various unpleasant deposits which he discovered upon his study floor and desk this morning, but I gather Mr Dick smoothed things over by telling him that 'everyone had a really good time and it would be a shame to spoil the leavers' last days with any bitterness over a few unfortunate excesses.'

And well he might say that! His willingness to cover up my own role in the affair was not entirely unconnected with our conversation at the end of last night, after I had discovered him in what some people might have described as a compromising position with Louise Scott, one of the sixth year's more mature – and stunningly attractive – members.

Frankly, I was appalled by what I saw, but reckoned his suggestion that we 'be mature about this, Morris, and I'll sort out that business over your conga-line' had much to commend it, lest Mr Tod vent his wrath on me.

In any case, I was more concerned this morning to get to the truth about the rumour currently sweeping the school which suggests that Rothesay Kyle and Alan McLeary have got engaged! Unfortunately, I couldn't query the couple themselves as they were both absent from school today – 'choosin' a ring, then gaun' tae an all-night rave', according to Tommy McShane, McLeary's erstwhile friend, as he collected his work-experience documentation from me this afternoon in readiness for his week at Mr Johnston's funeral parlour.

'Well good luck then, Tommy,' I bade him farewell, and was about to give him my usual work-experience speech about being polite to all the customers he'd be dealing with when I thought better of it, under the circumstances. 'So, um – all the best, then,' I concluded lamely.

'Thanks sur!' he smiled broadly. 'Ah'm really lookin' forward tae it!'

I sank back in my chair after he'd left and shook my head in bewilderment. How I longed for the presence of Mr Pickup for some friendly advice once more, but George Crumley robbed me of even that possibility at the afternoon interval.

'Pickup?' he answered my query about his non-appearance today. 'Got another furlough, I gather. Had his secondment extended by another four weeks to prepare a mission statement for regional policy on development plans.'

'A *what* statement?'

'A mission statement. A document that stops him working because he's busy writing down all the work he's going to do.'

'But he's always said these things are a complete waste of –'

'That's right,' Crumley confirmed. 'But he's been inside for eight weeks now, remember, and he's bound to have changed.'

'How d'you mean?' I queried anxiously.

'Seen it a hundred times,' Crumley explained. 'Once these people get inside the offices they suddenly find all sorts of things that need doing that have never been done before – and you suddenly wonder how on earth the education system ever managed to get along without them in the first place.'

I sighed loudly. The words could have belonged to Pickup himself only eight short weeks ago. *O tempora*, indeed ...

June

Times, and attitudes, had indeed changed since Morris Simpson had entered the teaching profession. For example, it would have been inconceivable for him to accept, at the outset of his career, that a pupil would ever swear at a teacher, let alone get away with it. Nevertheless, the lack of effective retribution towards Alan McLeary over his gross insult to Morris at the leavers' disco was simply one more symptom of an educational system in the midst of enormous attitudinal readjustment.

Some teachers, such as Mr Dunbar of maths, found it difficult to adjust to such changes and would increasingly seek early retirement. Other teachers, such as Matthew Gordon, would take solace in eternal, stress-related absences, thereby increasing the workload of their colleagues left behind in school. And other teachers still, such as Richard Dick, discovered that a more effective – and financially remunerative – remedy would be to shin up the promotional pole as fast as decency would allow, thereby removing themselves from the sordid necessity of engaging with pupils in the first place.

For promotion-seekers who found such channels of advancement blocked, however, there had recently arisen another avenue of escape, albeit a temporary one: the staff secondment. As we have already discovered, Mr Pickup had enjoyed his time in the regional offices, but was due back for the last week of term. Morris fully expected Pickup to confirm his previously-held beliefs that such secondments offered little or nothing to advance the cause of education other than a temporary respite from children and the chance to recharge one's mental barriers before re-entering the fray. Freedom once tasted, however, can be very sweet. It appeared to be a different David Pickup who returned from secondment that last week of term. For a time, Morris was worried. Very worried indeed.

Monday

Mr Pickup finally returned to school this morning after his twelve-week secondment as regional co-ordinator for forward development planning. I have been unnerved by the rumours concerning his changed personality, all of which testify to the fact that his hitherto cynical condemnation of such out-of-school activities has been replaced by a fervent enthusiasm to continue in his current post as a full time official rather than seconded teacher!

Unfortunately, I wasn't able to get him on his own this morning to check out the veracity of the rumours, and my fears weren't allayed when Richard Dick greeted him in the staffroom at lunchtime.

'Ah, David: nice to see you back,' oozed our depute head, whose own contact with educational innovation also tends to be at the distant remove of a few carefully-worded policy documents rather than in the daily context of classroom reality. As the conversation developed, it began to appear as if Pickup shared his sentiments as well.

'Good to *be* back, Dick,' Mr Pickup shook him by the hand. 'Although it was all a bit frustrating coming away like I did.'

'Oh?' Mr Dick leant forward sympathetically. 'How so, Mr Pickup? How so?'

'Well you know that mission statement I was developing for the region's approach to whole-school forward development plans?' asked Pickup.

'Indeed I do,' Dick nodded vigorously. 'Heard great things about it. Great things indeed.'

'Mm,' nodded Pickup. 'Well it was great so far as it went, but that was just the trouble. It didn't go far enough.'

'No?' sympathised Dick.

'No!' insisted Pickup firmly. 'What I could really have done with was another few months – or even a sabbatical year, maybe – to lick the thing into shape. I mean as it stands it's a fairly piece-meal approach which'll do fine as a set of guidelines, but we need a regionally co-ordinated policy of implementation to my mind, one which will really begin to –'

I couldn't believe what I was hearing. This was the man who has spent the last nine years advising me fiercely to shun such educational casuistry as if my sanity depended upon it, and here he was spouting forth like a walking policy document! I briefly interrupted his tedious monologue with a muttered 'Welcome back, Pickup,' but he barely found time to even acknowledge my presence before turning once again in the direction of Dick Dick and urging him to support his request for a further secondment next session.

I shook my head sadly and left the staffroom. I know when I'm not wanted.

Tuesday

Tommy McShane is still waxing lyrical – or as lyrical as a sub-literate 16-year old can get – about his work-experience last month at Mr Johnston's funeral parlour. Apparently, the five day secondment had the sole effect of reinforcing the boy's most earnest desire of becoming a mortician in adult life. Only this morning he was at me again to explore the career opportunities in the profession, and I have promised to do my best.

Meanwhile, final confirmation has been offered of last month's rumour concerning the engagement of Alan McLeary and Rothesay Kyle. Proof positive was provided by the touching sight of the betrothed pair arriving in school this afternoon to hand in a few remaining textbooks as well as show off their somewhat tawdry engagement ring to all and sundry. As their guidance teacher, I had the dubious honour of receiving the first such visitation.

'Um ... well – congratulations,' I stammered in some confusion, recalling only too clearly the sight of Alan McLeary when he arrived at Parkland High only four short years ago, as well as

Rothesay's arrival (as a school transfer) to second year just 30 months ago. And here they were, planning to get married!

'Thanks, sur!' beamed Rothesay, her hand linked firmly with McLeary's while he stood silently chewing gum. 'And thanks fur all yur help!'

'Oh – uh – don't mention it, Rothesay,' I replied. 'I presume your – uh – mother and – uh – stepfather are pleased about it as well?'

'Big Tony?' she scoffed. 'He's no' ma stepfather any mair, sur.'

'No?'

'Naw. He did a runner three months ago wi' a bird called Angela. Ma mammy's oan the look-out again.'

'Oh,' I stuttered in even greater confusion. 'I'm – uh – sorry to hear that, but – uh –'

'Ur y'interested, sur?' Rothesay smiled eagerly. 'She thinks you're smashin'!'

My face blushed scarlet, but before I could decline the offer, Rothesay had burst out laughing.

'Only jokin', sur! She likes ye, right enough, but she'd eat ye fur breakfast, so she would!'

'Hah!' I tried to join in with the joke before launching on a few well-chosen words of marital advice. Unfortunately, neither of them seemed predisposed to listen to my little pastoral homily, so I drew it to a swift conclusion by simply repeating my best wishes for the future as they sniggered together out of my office.

'Check, sur! Same tae you!' McLeary continued chewing his gum as he offered a valedictory wave. 'Play yer cards right, an' we might send ye an invite tae the weddin'!.'

I can only hope they don't.

Wednesday

I have still to speak to Mr Pickup alone: he has spent the past two days ensconced with Richard Dick, and apparently intent upon developing a customised mission statement for Greenfield Academy. It's all very sad.

Meanwhile, there is at least some good news on the Tommy McShane front. I have managed to locate a SCOTVEC module on undertaking, and it looks likely that Tommy will be accepted by Rockston College for a one-year vocational qualification which includes industrial placement and on-the-job experience leading to an eventual mortician qualification.

Tommy himself has not been idle, either: in yet another display of enthusiastic ingenuity, he told me this morning that he has managed to find a summer job at the Parkland crematorium.

'Well done, Tommy,' I congratulated him hesitantly. 'What as?'

'Crematorium assistant and sweeper, sur!' he said proudly.

'Oh, really?' I replied. 'So what'll you be sweeping, then? The paths? The funeral parlour?'

'Aye. Suppose so,' he shrugged his shoulders before an eager light came into his eyes. 'An' mebbe the ovens as well!'

'Yes. Well,' I gulped. 'Good luck with it, Tommy. Good luck indeed.'

'Thanks, sur. And thanks fur all yur help. Hope ah can help *you* sometime!'

'Well I hope not for a long time, Tommy,' I urged, in reference to his chosen future career, 'but thanks all the same. And give my regards to Rose,' I requested as he went out of the front door for the last time. 'Tell her my room's not been as tidy since she left, but I hope the bus conducting works out all right for her. I'm sure she's got the build for it ...'

Thursday

Mr Pickup has come clean! At last I managed to speak with him alone this morning, and asked him whether he actually *believed* any of the pronouncements I had heard tell of since his return. Secretively, he put one finger to his lips and told me 'Mum's the word, Simpson. The escape tunnel's half-way there!'

'So it *is* all a front!' I accused him triumphantly.

'Of course it is,' he whispered across the pigeon-holes. 'You didn't actually think I *meant* any of that mince, did you?'

'Well, it all sounded very convincing,' I had to admit.

'Good!' he smacked his lips together. 'If *you* were taken in, then it's obviously going to be no problem keeping it up with Dick Dick.'

Pressed further for some explanatory remarks, Pickup went on to explain that the regional office corridors are positively *bulging* with staff tutors, advisers and secondees such as himself.

'And all of them spewing out educational claptrap like there's no tomorrow!' he explained vigorously. 'And before long I found out just how easy it actually *is* to churn out that kind of stuff. It's like an accepted code of writing, light years away from plain English and largely meaningless: but very impressive to look at!' he emphasised sharply. 'And – this is the important bit, Morris –

when I actually get round to talking to them all, I discover they all feel exactly the same as me about it, and are only in there 'cos they've discovered that developing a quasi-educational prose style is the best means of escaping the classroom. And not one of them believes a bloody word of what they're writing in these endless mountains of verbiage! They're all in it together, and the Emperor's bloody clothes wouldn't have a look in!'

As if to prove his point, Mr Pickup withdrew a sheet of paper from his breast pocket. Excitedly, he started to pin it up on the staffroom noticeboard.

'Take a gander at this, Morris,' he encouraged me. 'It's all the rage in the offices. Under the counter, of course –'

Carefully, I squinted at the typewritten quotation he had placed on staffroom display. It read as follows:

'We trained hard but it seemed that every time we were beginning to form up into teams, we would be reorganised. I was to learn later in life that we tend to meet any new situation by reorganising, and a wonderful method it can be for creating the illusion of progress, while producing confusion, inefficiency and demoralisation.'
Caius Petronius, AD 66

Personally, I doubted the veracity of the quotation, but Pickup assured me of its legitimacy, and I had to admit, at least, its appropriateness to our current educational situation.

And it was certainly nice to know that Pickup was back to his old self, with me, at any rate. As far as Mr Dick's concerned, Pickup intends maintaining his front for as long as it takes to make good his permanent escape!

Friday

Last day of term, and an early finish this afternoon meant that Pickup and I could retire to The Rockston Arms for our annual review of the academic year.

It was, initially, a solemn occasion. Mr Dick had earlier made rather a fuss about Pickup's addition to the staffroom noticeboard, and had angrily torn it down, an action which Pickup had hypocritically commended as being 'exactly the right kind of response to make to whatever joker put it there'!

'Yes,' Mr Pickup commented in retrospect during our afternoon session. 'Dick actually looks as if he *does* believe in all of that crap I was talking about yesterday. I realised that after he'd ripped the notice down and started reading the riot act about rampant cynicism being so discouraging and demoralising for teachers like me! It's all a bit pathetic really, isn't it? But then so's school,' he added quietly.

Pickup's mood became even more sombre when I acquainted him with the future career prospects of selected fourth-year leavers.

'God almighty!' he exclaimed upon hearing of Tommy McShane's plans. 'It says a lot for Greenfield Academy if all we can prepare the likes of McShane for is a raging desire to become an undertaker, doesn't it! Mind you,' he reflected in introspective mood, 'if you ask me it's a wonder that any of them get into anything these days, what with the state of the country – not to mention the state of the education they've had. Anyone who actually succeeds in getting a job these days,' he pronounced decisively, 'probably does so in *spite* of anything we've taught them rather than because of it!'

I tried to cheer him up with the news of Alan McLeary and Rothesay Kyle, which I've actually come to accept by now.

'I mean it's quite sweet really, isn't it?' I suggested positively. 'Rothesay's had a pretty tough life to date, what with her home circumstances, so it's surely all to the good if she's found some happiness at last?'

For a moment, I thought Pickup was going to hit me.

'My God, Morris, haven't you learned *anything* in all these years? There's only one solution to families with problems like that' he emphasised frankly. 'And I think you know as well as I do that –'

I have heard Pickup before on his genetic solution of mass sterilisation for the lower orders, and refused to countenance such a discussion again. Instead, I repeated my contention that the possibility of Rothesay and Alan starting a family could make a big difference to them.

'Maybe,' I urged his support, 'it'll give the poor girl some kind of valid interest in life, what with –'

'Oh yes!' Pickup laughed sarcastically. 'It certainly will. But could I remind you, Morris, that Rothesay's current attention and interest span is approximately sixteen seconds, rapidly declining. By the time she's produced her obligatory six offspring by the age of 26 to demonstrate McLeary's virility; by the time she's discovered what it's like to actually look *after* them and consequently destroyed her few remaining brain cells with a regular diet of super-lager to get over the stress they induce; by the time McLeary's upped and left her for some other bint; or by the time she's upped and left *him* for some chancer she's met in a disco: by the time all *that's* over, d'you know who'll be left to pick up the pieces of that particular family?'

'Their social worker?' I queried tentatively.

'No, you daft bugger!' he swore angrily. 'Us! Her bloody kids' teachers! Just imagine it: what a bloody horrible thought when thirteen years from now Alan McLeary Junior turns up at the door for enrolment – I'll be long retired by then, but you won't Morris, and you'll soon find out the truth of what I've been telling you for years: the whole bloody thing just keeps going round in circles!'

It all seemed a particularly vituperative end to the academic year, so I tried to draw Pickup's attention to happier issues.

'Look, Pickup,' I cajoled him. 'Let's forget about Rothesay and McLeary, eh? Let's just look ahead to brighter things – like your mission statement, for example?'

In a trice he was back to his old self. 'Hah!' he laughed. 'You're right. If it all works out properly, why should I worry about anything? I shouldn't even be back in school *next* year if I play my cards right.'

'That's the spirit,' I patted him on the back before pondering the nature of his work in the regional offices. 'And tell me,' I queried, trying to keep his interest going, '– what's this mission statement all about anyway?'

Pickup stopped to think before breaking into a wide smile. 'My mission statement? Right now, Morris, it's got three objectives,' he explained patiently.

'Oh yes?' I nodded seriously.

'Yep. Long term, medium term and immediate term,' he drew a brief liquid diagram on the bar.

'I see.'

'In the long term, as you know, I plan to get a full time secondment in lieu of escaping the profession altogether. And in the medium term, I plan to have a bloody good summer holiday.'

'And your immediate term objective?' I questioned uselessly once more.

Pickup looked enquringly across the bar and raised his fingers. 'Two more pints?'

'You know, Mr Pickup,' I congratulated him on the suggestion. 'That's the best mission statement I've heard in the last twelve weeks.'

'Me too, Morris,' he congratulated himself. 'Me too. Fancy a chaser, by any chance?'

It was to be a long afternoon. And evening. But a great end to the term.

Postscript

As regular readers of the *Times Educational Supplement Scotland* will already know, Mr Pickup's subsequent attempts to attain a permanent secondment were severely frustrated during the opening months of the following academic session. And perhaps that was no bad thing.

As Morris Simpson has already commented within this – the fourth – volume of his school diaries culled from the pages of the aforementioned newspaper, David Pickup was probably happiest in front of a class, teaching pupils. It was a pity he seldom had the chance to do so. Teaching pupils, alas, comes low on a school's priority list these days.

There are endless initiatives to implement, a hundred forms to be filled in, new styles of assessment to be moderated, as well as weekly doses of policy-review which are required to be evaluated, found wanting and then re-introduced in a different guise some six months later.

But teachers like Morris Simpson and David Pickup still get by. They accept the edicts and the innovations from on high, trying valiantly to incorporate them into an overburdened curriculum whilst at the same time endeavouring to ensure that their implementation doesn't interfere *too* severely with the education of their young charges. For this, they are to be commended. Their occasional weariness, even cynicism, is perhaps understandable.

And what of the future? It would be a foolish person who would attempt to predict one for Scottish education, but there is one element which seems likely to prove more enduring than others, and that is the ongoing career, and irresistible rise, of Morris Simpson. Certainly, he has come farther already than his competence deserves. Alarmingly enough, I suspect he still has farther to go …

John Mitchell
July 1993